Lock Down Publications and Ca$h Presents

THE BIG HOMIE

BLINDED BY BLOOD

Written By

KING RIO

First Edition 2026

Printed in the United States of America

Lock Down Publications
P.O. Box 944
Stockbridge, GA 30281
www.lockdownpublications.com

Like our page on Facebook: Lock Down Publications
www.facebook.com/lockdownpublications.ldp

Stay Connected with Us!

Text **LOCKDOWN** to 22828 to stay up-to-date with new releases, sneak peaks, contests and more…

Like our page on Facebook:
Lock Down Publications

Join Lock Down Publications/The New Era Reading Group

Visit our website:
www.lockdownpublications.com

Follow us on Instagram:
Lock Down Publications

Email Us: We want to hear from you!

Prologue

Blood in the Snow

"Get off of me!"

Vielle shoved away from Trey and went sprinting into the narrow hall with her mind set on locking herself in the bathroom. It was a notably short distance of just seven or eight feet. She could make it there in less than two seconds, and she did, only Trey got a handful of her radiant red hair just as she closed her hand on the aluminum doorknob.

"Bitch!" He yanked and at the same time reached around to clamp his free hand around her throat. "You wanna flirt with niggas on Facebook? You wanna leave heart eyes under niggas pictures and shit? That's what you wanna do? Huh, bitch? Huh, bitch?"

His powerful grip cut off her airway, making her eyes bulge from their sockets. He pressed his forehead against hers and sneered in her face. A harsh choking sound issued forth from her throat. She managed a small nasal intake of air and smelled the weed and cognac on his breath.

"I'll kill you, Vee. You hear me? I will choke you to death in this bitch. Stop fuckin' playin' with me."

Vielle couldn't ptalk at all, but she could move just fine. She shot her knee up into Trey's groin and struck gold. He inhaled sharply and instantly relinquished his hold on her neck as he fell to his knees, both hands moving toward the fresh source of pain between his thighs. Vielle threw two hard hooks that connected on the left and right sides of his jaw, and she didn't stick around to see him topple over onto his side. She darted back into the living room wearing nothing but the black-and-red pajama pants and plain black tee she'd put on after her shower, and after snatching up her purse from the coffee table and hastily slipping into her Nike running shoes, she ripped open the apartment door and rushed out into a snowstorm.

Treykwan Murray, aka Trey, lived in a one-bedroom apartment with his big brother, Bryshon "Thirty" Perry. They had the same daddy and different mamas. Thirty was a fat black thirty-year-old weed-dealer with a rapper's eye for fashion. He'd been bagging up individual grams of Pink Runtz, an exotic strain of marijuana he purchased by the bale, when Trey hauled off and slapped Vielle across the face as she'd sat on the living room sofa on her iPhone, swiping through TikTok videos. Thirty had looked up from the dining room table seven feet away when he heard the smack, and then he'd returned his focus to the chunky clumps of weed on his digital scale.

Running out the apartment door, Vielle was hit by a frigid sheet of snowy wind that stung her face almost as much as that ear-ringing slap. Icy flakes of snow poured down at an angle, making her squint as she ran up the concrete path to the parking lot out front. She dug in her purse as she fled, first grabbing her .45-caliber Springfield XD pistol and then snagging her keys. She owned the jet black BMW coupe that was parked closest to the end of the footpath. It sat directly beside Thirty's matte black Suburban. He had tinted windows and enormous rims on the SUV, gold 32-inch Forgiatos. Vielle loved riding in the Suburban with him, something the two of them had been doing a lot more often over the past five weeks or so that he'd been crashing on the foldout bed in Trey's living room sofa.

Vielle hated him for not stepping into the fight on her behalf.

She started the engine remotely and was just pulling her driver door shut when Trey emerged from the dense fog of snow, all six feet three inches of him. Dark and willowy, he ran bare-chested through the cold. His alcohol-infused blood warming his heavily tatted torso melted the snowflakes as they lit on his skin.

"Vee, if you don't get the fuck back in there!" he shouted.

But Vielle was already backing out of the parking space. She couldn't see out of her left eye — that eye was dead, just a smoky gray pupil trapped inside a brighter gray iris — but her light hazel right eye had 20/20 vision, and that was all she needed. She was throwing her leather-bound steering wheel into a spin, whipping her car around to speed off out of the parking lot entrance, when Trey appeared at her door with his fist drawn back to punch through her closed window.

Vielle stepped down on the brake pedal while simultaneously raising the gun from her lap. A flick of her thumb switched on a green laser beam that she trained on Trey's throat.

"Go 'head! Go 'head and do it! I dare you!" Vielle's face still stung where she'd been slapped. Hot tears of anger and hurt removed the remaining snowflakes from her strawberry brown cheeks. "Bust my window and see what the fuck I do, bitch. See what the fuck I do."

Trey pulled up short. For a brief moment he stood frozen in place with his long naked arm folded back past his shoulder. Then he nodded his not-so-handsome head a couple of times, flitted his eyes around the well-lit but desolate parking lot, and finally flashed his teeth in a vicious little sneer as he reached behind his back. His hand returned to view holding the Glock 22 that Vielle had bought him for his twenty-fifth birthday two months ago, a .40-caliber handgun with a 22-round extended magazine. They were a part of the generation that put guns and fashion above the hustle, and so she'd gifted him the gun and three pairs of Jordans.

And now Trey was turning that very same gun on her.

She squeezed the trigger and shot him without a moment's hesitation. The green dot had moved to his right shoulder by then, and that tiny green dot became a dime-sized bullet wound two milliseconds before the blood poured forth. More blood misted out of his back, coloring the snowfall behind him as he jerked rearward. His gun flipped out of his hand, went skidding across the slushy ground, and vanished beneath a parked Toyota SUV. The bullet punched a big hole in Vielle's window, and the cold air swept in to chill her warmly flowing tears.

There was a glitch in her memory after that. One second she was there in that south side parking lot, and the next she was pulling into the driveway next to her close friend Bambi's west side home. She remembered grabbing her iPhone 17 Pro from the carpeted floor in front of Trey's pungent brown sofa, and she figured she'd called Bambi sometime during that memory lapse. Bambi was standing in the open doorway when Vee got out of the car — nose running, teeth chattering, mind racing a mile a minute — and ran up the porch steps into her arms.

"I j-j-just sh-shot him," Vielle confessed to her closest confidant in the entire town. She was sobbing and stuttering and shivering, and she knew her face must have felt like ice against the sensuous warmth of Bambi's caramel brown cheek. "I sh-shot that w-woman-beatin' sonofabitch right in his n-narrow ass chest. He m-made me do it. He pulled a gun on me."

"Girl, come on in out of this cold. I'll fix you a drink."

Bambi locked the door and led Vielle through the living room and dining room to a modest-sized kitchen with vinyl tile flooring and relatively new looking granite countertops. The air was heavily redolent of chicken, and Vee saw several fried drumsticks in a strainer next to the stove. Bambi left the room and returned seconds later with a yellow-and-orange checkered quilt that she draped around Vielle's shoulders. She poured up twin shots of tequila while Vee gave her the rundown.

"I liked a couple of Baby Gang's pictures on Facebook. That's all I did, sis. I swear 'fore God, that's all the fuck I did."

"The pictures of him on the basketball court with Meko and Shaggy n'em?"

"Yeah, those."

"Bitch, he was too damn fine. I went through every picture he posted, liked every one of em," Bambi said, lowering her meaty rump onto the chair across from Vee's. She was a pretty girl, brown-skinned like the chicken in the strainer, with full lips and lustrous black hair that was currently fashioned into braids. She leaned forward on her forearms. "So Trey flipped out over that? To the point where you had to pop his stupid ass?"

Vee nodded twice and threw back the shot, which instantly warmed her to the core. "He slapped the fuck outta me. I mean, that's the hardest I've ever been hit in my life! My first boyfriend was highly abusive, beat on me at least twice a week until my brother Lorde flew down to Houston and beat him down in front of the whole neighborhood, but Marvell ain't never hit me as hard as Trey smacked me tonight. And then he chased me up the hallway and choked me until I 'bout passed out. I had to kick him in the nuts to get him up off of me. Then I hit him with a mean ass two piece and got the fuck up outta there. I was backin' out to leave when he ran up on my car with his fist balled up like he was about to punch right through my window, so I upped my pistol and dared him to do it. Instead of swinging he reached back and pulled out the gun I bought him for his birthday, so I shot him in the shoulder. Made him drop the gun. Then I drove off. I think I took Southwind Drive to South Court and then took Ohio all the way over here to the west side, and with a broken window at that."

The tears were still flowing, but a childish little giggle escaped Vielle's throat at the memory of her small fists crashing against both sides of Trey's jaw. She was born in Chicago but raised in Houston, Texas, in the economically disadvantaged Third Ward neighborhood where fistfights were an everyday occurrence, but Vee had never been much of a fighter herself. That being said, she was quite proud of herself for the two swift hooks she'd thrown at Trey. She thought Claressa Shields might have given her a standing ovation for that stellar boxing performance.

"Do you think he could've died?" Bambi asked as she got up and came around the ash wood table to hug Vielle from behind; apparently she felt this question required a large dose of human contact.

Vee shrugged her shoulders. "Probably not. I should've. His ass is lucky my daddy wasn't there."

"Oh yeah, that's right, Hard gets out of prison this week. I forgot all about that."

Vielle sniffed and chortled and shook her head, thinking of her dear father and the beating he would have put on Trey for laying hands on his baby girl.

"He'll be home in less than twenty-four hours," she said, her words coated in an icy kind of joy. "Let's see what he thinks about Trey slapping me across my face and choking me like that." She nodded again and winced against the dull ache in her throat. "Yeah. We'll see how niggas act when my daddy come home."

Chapter 1

"Big homie, don't forget about me. I know you about to get out there and get to the bag. Don't forget about lil bro. I still got all day in this bitch."

"I'll never forget about you, shorty. On my kids."

Hard put an arm around Bo's shoulder and gave him a squeeze. The two of them were sitting side by side on the bunk Hard had slept in for the past twelve years.

They were in cell 311, on C-East in C-Cell House at Indiana State Prison, the correctional institution Hardis had lived in since he was transported from the Laporte County Jail in December of 2006. He'd done another year there in county lockup, fighting a murder charge that he honestly knew nothing about.

There were a dozen others lingering in the open doorway and on the range outside his cell. All of them were upstanding members of the Almighty Vice Lord Nation. Bo and Hard were both lifelong members themselves — Hard a high-ranking Traveling Vice Lord, Bo a lower ranking Conservative Vice Lord. For more than a decade Bo and Hard had been the closest of friends. They'd made a few hundred thousand dollars dealing drugs and cell phones inside the prison, and they'd crushed everybody who ever got in their way.

The grisly scar in Bo's left jawline came from a particularly bloody knife fight they'd had with a group of Gangster Disciples.

But those days were officially over. All of Hard's mail and books were packed, and he'd handed out the rest of his property to the less fortunate. In just four hours, at the stroke of midnight, he'd be walking out the front gates of ISP a free man.

The bros outside his cell were shouting over the three huge bags of commissary food he'd given them to split amongst themselves.

"I'm leaving you this phone," Hard said, taking his iPhone 14 Pro out of his sweatpants pocket and handing it to Bo.

Bo took the phone in one veiny black hand and tightened his fist around it. He was as strong as an ox and short as a fox, maybe five-four, certainly no taller than five-five. He'd only been growing his dreads for three years and already they were down past his shoulders. He was sitting with his elbows on his knees and his head hanging forward, and Hard got the feeling that there were tears of real despair falling under those hairy black ropes, tears that Bo wanted no one but Allah to see.

Hard got up and ushered everyone else out of the cell, but neither man strayed more than five feet away; they would stand there on the range with knives in their waistbands and their eyes on every prisoner who happened to wander past Hard's cell. He shut his makeshift curtain — a gray wool blanket on a string — to give Bo the words he'd been waiting until this very day to give him.

"I pulled Officer Jones when I went to the hole in August," Hard said, taking another iPhone from his other sweatpants pocket. This one was a 16 Pro Max, and he was planning on taking it home. "She gon' start bringing you a pack every other weekend. Ounces of ice, weed, and tobacco, cell phones and smart watches. Just pay her three bands every move and she'll keep the shit comin'. You good with that?"

Bo looked up at Hard. Small wet circles dotted the smooth gray concrete floor between his tan Timberland boots. His eyes were red and teary, but his expression was stunned.

"Miss Jones?" Bo said incredulously. "Sexy ass Miss Jones from Chicago? She the one been bringing you all that shit?"

Hard nodded hesitantly. "Yeah," he said and paused, thinking of what might happen to Katoya Jones and her young daughter if it ever got out that she was trafficking drugs and phones into the prison. "Yeah, but don't tell nobody the play, and I mean nobody at all. Just sell that shit, pay her, and FaceTime me so I can get you some more."

Bo was clearly distraught over Hard's imminent departure from his everyday life, but the prospect of having his own drug mule brightened his mood significantly. He wiped his face and stood up smiling, eagerly accepting the brotherly hug Hard had for him.

"Love, lil bro. Undyin' Love," Hard said, patting Bo on the back. "I gotchoo. Just be patient, give me a couple weeks to get settled in out there. I got plans, Bo. Big plans. You just wait and see."

Chapter 2

Hard was given a folded pile of brand-new clothes when he walked into the shift office four hours later. It was the outfit his youngest son, Lorde, had delivered days ago for him to wear home. A black hoodie with the word AMIRI emblazoned across the chest in puffy gold lettering and black jeans by the same designer. The shoes were black-and-gold Jordan 5's.

"He brought you a coat, too," Lieutenant Angela Witt told me. She was a skinny brown older woman from Memphis, Tennessee. One gold canine tooth twinkled in her simpering smile. Aside from her there were four more DOC employees in the shift office and one elderly inmate worker mopping the floor. One officer gave Hard a friendly wave goodbye, and the geriatric janitor offered him a shaky-handed salute. Witt glowered at the old man and said, "Lewis, you need to be moppin' this goddam floor." Then her smile returned and she pointed Hard toward the changing area he'd been strip-searched in before and after every visit with his family and friends. "Your coat's in there. It's a black bubble coat, real nice lookin' too. You gon' like it."

He nodded and went, and no one escorted him there. He'd figured as much. There weren't many inmates who passed through the shift office at night besides those who were officially free men. Plus, Hard knew this was Lt. Witt's shift, and she'd been crushing on him for years.

No escort meant that it was easy transferring the iPhone from his boxer-briefs to the inside pocket of his Moncler coat. He was dressed in seconds. His heart pounded like concert speakers as he walked back out of the saloon-like swinging doors and back out into the shift office.

His mesh bag full of books weighed maybe sixty pounds. He yanked the string tight and threw the bag over his shoulder.

"Good luck out there, Hard," Witt said as she walked him through a door that had previously been off-limits to him. "You stay yo' butt outta trouble, ya hear me? I don't wanna see you back in here for violating parole. Give them white folks their two years and go on about your business."

"I'll never come back," Hard said, meaning it with all his heart.

The lieutenant moved aside when they went through the next sliding door, and Hard found himself in a wide, yellow-linoleum-tiled hallway with a slender cobalt carpet that ran straight out to a set of double doors. There were big rectangular panes of glass in the doors through which he could see the halfway deserted parking lot. Only one door was open. Cold air swept in and chilled his lungs.

It was the most refreshing breath of air he'd inhaled in all his forty-four years of living.

He stepped outside and laid eyes on his 39-year-old girlfriend, Tazera "Candy" Williams, and all four of his adult children — 28-year-old Hardis Laray Gaing Jr, 26-year-old Flower Patrice Gaing, 22-year-old Lorde James Gaing, and 21-year-old Vielle Golden Gaing.

The Gaings.

His four kids stood beaming beside Lorde's smoke-gray Jeep Grand Cherokee Trackhawk. Idling ahead of it was another SUV, the white Dodge Durango SRT he'd had delivered to Candy's suburban home on her birthday last September.

Candy ran to him as he walked to her. Her complexion was like pure honey on fresh wheat bread, and her heart was just as pure and sweet. Her eyes were bright brown, not far from hazel, and her lips were so full that they could have been collagen-injected. Candy was tall for a woman, five-ten without shoes, but she didn't seem all that tall standing in front of Hard. He had to lower his head and lean in to kiss her juicy lips.

Hard was and always had been a big man. Six feet five inches of almond brown skin wrapped around two hundred and sixty pounds of solid muscle. His beard was as thick as his Chicago accent and his head was bald; he'd shaved it smooth and oiled his naked scalp just two hours ago. He'd met Candy on Facebook in early 2021, and ever since then she'd been traveling from her home on the western outskirts of Indianapolis to visit him every two weeks.

"You got one hour with them, Hard," Candy whispered hungrily in his ear. His hands were overly busy, squeezing her soft jiggly butt through her skintight blue jeans, but his ears heard her every word. "One hour. That's all I'm allowing. After that it's me and you."

"You already know, baby."

She moved aside after that, her red leather bomber jacket standing out with brilliant clarity in the dark of night.

Hard approached his kids and smiled joyfully at the four pairs of arms that closed around him all at once. His oldest boy, HJ, was generally disliked by his siblings — he was a cop, a real-deal homicide detective, and the majority of the Gaings hated cops — but in this particular moment there was no animosity between the brothers and sisters, just tearful joy at the fact that their father was free after spending two full decades in the slammer.

"Come on," Vielle said, "let's get away from this prison before they find a reason to kidnap you again."

"We cooked you some steaks like you asked," Flower said. She was an inch or two shorter than Candy. Many people opined that she was really just a taller version of Vielle. "Steak, baked potatoes, mac and cheese, burgers, fries, chicken, spaghetti, greens, barbecue ribs. The works."

Hard's stomach chose that very moment to growl and he salivated at the thought of all that good food, all that real food, just sitting there at Vielle's house waiting for him to sit down and devour it.

"I'm finna eat'bout three plates," he said, rubbing his belly. "Yeah, let's get over there right now. We'll sit down and talk when we get there."

"No, we'll talk on the way there." Vielle was climbing up into the backseat of the Durango, while Flower made herself comfortable in the front passenger seat and Candy hurried around to the driver door.

Hard took a step back to shake hands with his sons and study their attire. This proved to be a study in polar opposites. HJ wore a navy blue blazer with MCPD printed across the back in big yellow block letters over plain gray slacks and black leather dress shoes. He was six three and a half, slim with a notable element of athleticism, and his eyes were the hazel that Candy's aspired to be.

On the other hand, Lorde was pitch black with white diamond encrusted platinum teeth and long dreadlocks that were bound together in wicks. Hard didn't know the brand of clothing Lorde was wearing, but he knew that the light blue jeans and the dark gray sweatshirt Lorde wore under his open gray jacket were high-end designer because high-end designer was all Lorde wore. It was the way Hard had dressed as a crack and heroin dealer before prison, and so it came as no surprise when Lorde started supporting himself the same way, a life of excess financed by the plentiful profits of the dope game. Lorde was an unsigned underground rap artist called Rap Lorde who used the money he got from trafficking and dealing in large quantities of high-grade bud to bolster his music career; Hard knew this for certain, Vielle and Flower knew it too, and they all knew better than to share that incriminating information with HJ.

"It's good to see you, son," Hard said to HJ.

HJ ran a hand forward over the waves of hair he'd brushed into intricate spirals all around his head. "Good to see you too, old man." He stuffed his hands in the pockets of his blazer. "I'm working a case right now, and my car's parked back there" — one hand came out to thrust a thumb over his shoulder — "but I'll see you sometime tomorrow...well, today."

A drab chuckle ensued and then HJ was gone, jogging off toward his royal blue Ford Explorer. Hard noted the Glock he wore holstered on his hip as he went, and the gold badge that identified him as MCPD Homicide Detective Hardis L. Gaing Jr.

"Weird ass nigga," Lorde muttered indignantly. He walked around to the driver's side of his shiny gray Trackhawk with his face twisted in abject disgust. "Pops, you ridin' with me. And get in the back. The bros put you a nice lil welcome home package together for you. It's all in that bookbag."

Hard yanked open the rear passenger's side door and got in and pulled the door back shut in one fluid motion. The temperature outside had to be in the mid thirties; not exactly freezing, but far from warm. His hairless scalp needed warmth, so he hardly paid any mind to the brown leather Louis Vuitton backpack on the seat beside him. It took Lorde's urging to get him to open it, and that was after they'd turned onto Willard Avenue, a few blocks down from the prison.

"Open up that book bag," Lorde said. "Take a look in there. How many niggas you know get out the joint to that kinda bag."

Lorde's emphasis on the word 'that' compelled Hard to unzip the backpack, and what he glimpsed inside it made his mouth fall wetly open. There was a diamond watch, a thick diamond chain with a diamond pendant that spelled out his nickname, HARD, in big capital letters, and numerous piles of cash all rubber-banded together.

"Millionaire Markio bought you that chain and gave you fifty thousand," Lorde said. "Bam bought you the watch and gave you twenty thousand. Luke gave you ten, Ola gave you ten, and I threw ten racks in there to make it a even hundred thousand. Look in that side pocket too."

Hard unzipped the second compartment and removed the contents, a black key fob and an iPhone 17 Pro Max, the latter of which reminded him that he still hadn't turned on the iPhone he had in his coat pocket.

"I wanted to go in on the car with Markio but you know he got that Hollywood movie money now. He paid for it in cash."

"What kinda car is it?"

Lorde looked back at Hard and smiled at him, that was it. No verbal answer was to come. There was a logo on the key fob that looked kind of like a bird's wings put together to form a V, but Hard had no idea what kind of car the key went to.

"I know you probably didn't notice with all the makeup Vielle got on, but her lil boyfriend slapped her last night. Choked her too. She got a handprint on the left side of her face and some bruises on her neck."

It's amazing how fast murderous rage can arise from a single revelation.

"And what the fuck did y'all do about it?" Hard bellowed.

"You know me and Flower live in Chicago. I ain't find out about that shit until we got here today. She say she shot the nigga in his shoulder, and now he been sendin' threats, sayin' he gon' shoot up the crib. I'm just tellin' you 'cause that's where you gon' be livin'. Vee didn't want me to tell you."

For several long seconds Hard stared at the side of his youngest son's head and didn't speak. Some idiot had chosen to lay hands on his baby girl, and as much as he loathed the idea of violating parole and heading back to prison before he even made it to his first parole office check-in, there was no way he would allow some coward boyfriend of Vee's to get away with choking and slapping her. He wouldn't be able to look himself in the mirror if he let such an egregious violation go unchecked.

"What's his name?" Hard asked, powering on his iPhone 16. "Vielle's boyfriend. I want his name."

"They call him Trey. He ain't on shit, Pops. She shot buddy in the shoulder, made him drop his glizzy and everything. The nigga sendin' threats from a hospital bed. He ain't nobody to worry about."

"Who he run with?"

"It's usually Trey and Thirty, they brothers, and they got some homies they be with too. Some BD's. Thirty the face card. He just bought sixty pounds'a Pink Runtz from me a few weeks ago. He got a big-ass crib under renovation somewhere in Chicago Heights, but he been ducked off with Trey in some projects out here called Southgate. That's where the whole fight between Vee and Trey went down. From what she told me, they fought in his apartment and she shot him in the parking lot."

"You got Thirty's number?"

Lorde gave Hard the number and he texted it immediately. Told Thirty to FaceTime him, and that he was Vielle's pops. He had just hit send when he got a FaceTime call from the daughter in question.

Her pie-shaped visage was so incredibly beautiful. Even with the dead eye. She'd moved here to Michigan City from Houston in April just to get a house for Hard to parole to. She beamed at him and he studied her face, searching for bruising, swelling, anything.

"Why you lookin' at me like that?" Her smile dimmed and her brow wrinkled.

"What's up with Trey?" Hard asked in a tone that was nowhere near as neutral as he'd intended it to be.

"Bro, you a rat," Vielle said to the brother she couldn't see.

Lorde replied, "Don't get beat up, lil girl."

"What's up with Trey?" Hard asked again.

"He's at Saint Anthony's. Or at least he was. I think Thirty and Big Block was supposed to be going to get him sometime tonight. I saw it on Thirty's IG Story."

Flower took the phone. "Daddy, we good. Everybody's staying at her house with you tonight. Lorde got Lil Luke, Fayzo, and Baby Lord over there, and they got all kinda guns. We are good, you hear me? No worries whatsoever."

"Forget all that," Vielle said, snatching the phone back. "You free, Daddy. Free as a bird. We ain't about to let no nigga throw off our vibes. My daddy free after twenty years. It's up."

They all laughed and cheered at that. Vielle had that sort of effect on people. She knew how to make you smile through the rain. A few months back her face had been plastered all over CNN, the victim of an alleged kidnapping by one of America's most wanted fugitives — 83-year-old Herbert Harris, a Vietnam war veteran known for killing his enemies with C4 explosives, the sword in his cane, and his trusty old Winchester sniper rifle. Even so, Vee had sounded cheery as ever when she FaceTimed Hard three days after the alleged kidnapping from a Spanish-style villa in Matamoros, Mexico.

"Papi's Place" is what they called that sprawling 400-acre estate just across the border from Brownsville, Texas. There were two nightclubs, a 30-car underground parking garage, and a gambling parlor toward the forefront of the property, and behind that was the 50,000-square-foot villa. Papi's Place was once owned by Juan "Papi" Costilla, a deceased former boss of the infamous Matamoros Cartel, but now it was just another hotel resort streamlined to the public under the ownership of Costilla Corp. Papi was long dead and now his daughter, Alexus Costilla-King, was in charge. She had a legitimate net worth of $497 billion, and there was no telling how much more she'd raked in from her paternal family's drug cartel. Hard had bought hundreds of bricks of cocaine from Papi himself, in the early days when Alexus was just a pretty little mixed girl who trailed along behind Hard whenever he came to visit her daddy. Seeing his own little girl there at Papi's Place while he sat helpless in a prison cell had humbled him in a way that must be experienced to be understood.

"I'm good, Daddy," Vielle had told him that day. "I'm way down here in Matamoros, sipping caipirinhas by the pool. Your guy Herb introduced me to some real (and this part she'd whispered) real Mexican drug cartel niggas. They're hiding us out here at this resort. Daddy, they bought me a BMW coupe and gave me a house on the west side of Michigan City for you to live in when you come home in December. I even saw Alexus here once. Didn't get to meet her, but I saw her. I saw her pull up. It was like fifteen white Rolls-Royces. I know people think Herb kidnapped me or whatever, but that old man actually saved my life. He's sending me back to Indiana on a private jet!"

The luminous smile Vielle had worn that day was on her face now. Hard looked away from his phone screen and stared vacantly out his window. There were too many thoughts charging through his head. A hundred percent freedom after twenty years of incarceration was another one of those things that couldn't be understood without suffering through the experience. The best way he could describe it is that it's like having a real F5 tornado churning through your chest, only instead of tossing up cars and houses this tornado whipped up raw, soul-gripping emotion. Grin-inducing emotion.

And man was he grinning.

"Daddy, I ain't never seen you this happy," Vielle noted, which sent Hard's eyes on a journey from his window, down into the LV backpack to briefly ogle all those corpulent stacks of cash, and finally back to his phone screen to look Vielle in the eye.

"I don't think I ever been this happy in my life. You know how long I been gone. Now I got all this bread Lord n'em just gave me, and I still got a hundred and ninety in the bank. I just came home a three-hundred-thousand-dollar nigga. First day out."

"Three hundred thousand? That was Candy. "Uhhh, where is all that at? Because you told me that the twenty-three thousand you got in my bank account was all you had. You been hiding money? That's what we on?"

Hard laughed and didn't say a word. His daughters laughed too, and Candy giggled like a schoolgirl.

"She must not know about Hardis Laray Gaing Senior," Vielle said in her delightfully cheerful tone of voice. Her hair was red and lustrous, matching her crimson lips. "My daddy holds his money close, Candy. Only the family type shit. He done bought me four cars since I started driving, he got Flower that Tesla and two different Tahoes, and he even bought Lorde that black BMW 760 he used in his first few music videos, but other than us the only people he ever spent money on was my mama and my grandma. That's how we knew he really liked you, when he bought you this truck..."

Vielle went on talking to the gorgeous young woman who'd spent every other weekend with Hard in the visiting room at Indiana State Prison. He set the phone down on his lap and fastened the diamond watch around his left wrist. It was a platinum Rolex Sky Dweller replete with twinkling white VVS diamonds. He'd seen that kind of watch before — in magazines like Kite and Go Viral during his time in prison, and on the wrists of rap stars in music videos he'd watched on YouTube — but never had he thought that he'd have an icy watch of his own and a chain and pendant to go with it before he even made it home.

Home came two blocks later. It was a two-story burgundy clapboard house smack-dab in the middle of 7th Street. Willard Avenue ran past the nearest corner. He consulted his mental map of the area and realized with growing displeasure that the homicide he'd gone down for had taken place just around the corner from where he would likely be living until his two years of parole was completed. He'd fought in court to have his parole switched over to Chicago, but the Interstate Compact was ultimately denied and he was ordered to reside in Laporte County, Indiana, at least until he was released from parole.

He put on his chain and gawked at the candy red Chevy Corvette that was parked beside Vielle's BMW coupe on the smoothly paved concrete driveway that ran from the curb to the side of his new home address. The first thing he noticed was that the Corvette had the same winged emblem as his key fob. Next his attention went to the gold rims, and then he studied the other vehicles that were parked at the curb. If not for the driveway leading to their garage, they'd have had to park down at the far end of the block, because there were no vacant spaces along the curb on their end.

Lorde pulled in behind Vee's M6 and parked. "I know you on parole, Pops, but you gon' need a gun stayin' out here with Vee. Dude might come over here after I go back home. I don't really know nobody out here. Ain't no tellin' what they gon' try to pull."

"My girl got a gun in her purse at all times, a fat ass Glock 26. I'll empty the clip and won't think twice about it if I got to, but that's not what I'm on. I'm spreading love, son. Love, truth, peace, freedom, and justice. You feel me, baby boy?"

Lorde bobbed his head. "That's all good with me, but I ain't going for no goofy shit. If Trey and his guys let a single shot off at this house I'm spinnin' on em."

Hard stepped out of the backseat with the backpack on one shoulder and his mesh bag full of books on the other. His gaze drifted back to the Corvette, its cherry red paintwork shimmering with tiny little golden flakes. A lump formed in his throat, and for a moment he forgot about the concrete and steel that had defined his past two decades. He forgot about all the lost years, the missed birthdays, and the hollow ache of having to father his children from a distance.

Lorde's voice broke the spell: "So what's the verdict? You like it or not?"

Hard's eyes snapped to his son, and a slow smile spread across his face. "Like it? Man, this is...wow." He shook his head, chuckling. "Y'all didn't have to do all this."

Lorde grinned. "Yeah we did. You're home now. We been waitin' on this day for way too long."

Hard's chest swelled with a mixture of pride and gratitude. He hadn't been much of a father to Lorde, not by his own standards. But the kid was giving him a chance to make up for all the time he'd missed out on, a chance to be the father God had created him to be.

The house was dark. Hard saw light in only one window, toward the back of the house. As the five of them went up the porch steps, the front door swung open, and a tiny voice squealed, "Daddy! Daddy's home!"

Hard's head snapped up, and his heart skipped a beat. A little girl, no more than five, was bounding down the steps, her curly hair bouncing with every step. Hard's face went slack. For a moment he forgot to breathe.

Lorde chuckled. "That's your granddaughter, Pops. My daughter, Journee."

It was at that exact moment when all the house lights seemed to turn on at once.

"Surprise!"

Scooping up his daughter in one arm, Lorde ushered Hard into the living room where a good twenty of his closest friends and relatives stood cheering with smiles on their faces and smartphones in their hands. His mother, Vella, and her sister, Vicky, were among the many beaming faces. Colorful "Welcome Home" balloons hung from the clean white walls. Unopened bottles of liquor lined the cherry wood coffee table. An 80-inch widescreen TV began playing Al Green's classic "Love and Happiness."

As the hugs came, Hard's vision blurred, and he felt the weight of the past two decades bearing down on him. He swept his Mama up in his arms and held her tightly.

"Welcome home, Pops," Lorde said, clapping him on the back.

Hard nodded, his voice catching in his throat. "I'm home, family," he said. "I'm finally home."

Chapter 3

Trey hadn't said much since returning to his small and rather nicely furnished apartment.

He had winced as Thirty and Big Block assisted him in gently lowering himself onto the living room sofa. The intense ache in his shoulder had receded quite a bit, thanks in huge part to the two twenty-milligram Percocets he'd swallowed down before leaving the hospital an hour ago.

That medicinal effect made him comfortable enough to think through his issues with his girlfriend, Vielle Gaing.

Girlfriend or not, someone was going to pay for the hole in his shoulder.

"Li'l bro, you just need to kick back for a couple'a weeks," Thirty advised as he stood across the room with his fat black arms folded across his chest. His hair was two or three inches long and braided in two-strand twists that were fast becoming dreads. His light gray sweater was just as impeccably clean as his light blue jeans and fresh gray Timberland boots. The sweater was made by Dior and therefore exorbitantly priced — $1,989.99 to be exact — but prices rarely ever mattered to Thirty. He dragged an obese knot of cash out of his right-hand pocket. "We can pay one'a them li'l niggas a band or two to get that shit done while you sit back and heal up."

"Shiiiit, you can give that two thousand dollars to me," Big Block said. "I'll swing through there and do that shit myself."

Thirty shook his head no. Trey's hard brown eyes fluctuated from Big Block to Thirty and back to Big Block, who was six feet six inches tall and far too clumsy to send on a drill. He might have had the height of a pro hooper but there was nothing athletic about Derrick "Big Block" Tyson. Whether standing or sitting, his top half was always stooped forward, as if he suffered from scoliosis, and he walked at a sluggish pace. Trey had never seen him run anywhere. He couldn't imagine sending Big Block on a mission of any kind, let alone an important one.

Big Block sat down at the opposite end of the sofa and slouched back like a lazy man, looking at the 65-inch widescreen TV. Tyler Perry's "The Oval" was playing on the screen. Trey didn't much care for the show, but Vielle loved it, and they'd watched several seasons of the primetime political drama over the past couple of months.

"Hard texted me a lil while ago." Thirty took out his phone. "Asked me to FaceTime him. I think he got out at around midnight. You know that's when ISP release niggas who goin' home." He stared down at something on his phone screen. Trey discerned a certain degree of reluctance on his older brother's face, and he wasn't at all surprised when Thirty looked up and added, "Man, we gotta try to dead this situation. I know Vee might be your girl or whatever, but her brother is my plug, and her daddy — shit, you know about that nigga. You heard the same stories I done heard. Hard is a cold-blooded gangsta. How many times Uncle Ray done told us about all the wild shit Hard did back in the day? And you wanna start some shit wit' this nigga?!"

"I remember Hard," Block said, his voice so deep that it could have risen from the bottom of a wine barrel. "He definitely was standin' on business. That nigga had them bricks, and if he fronted you some weight and you didn't pay, yo' ass was as good as dead. I guarantee you, wherever he at right now, he got a bankroll on him and some niggas that'll kill for him. Especially Lorde and his niggas. You know how crazy them Chicago rap niggas is. We really need to be tryna link up with them niggas, get some money...but if you dead set on shootin' up Vee's crib I'll go through there and do that shit right now. Just be ready for the consequences."

Trey still didn't speak. He was wearing a vapid blue hoodie with Givenchy printed across the chest in gray block letters. His sweatpants matched the hoodie. Four years of hair growth had his dreadlocks down to his chest. His right shoulder was all bandaged up under his hoodie and the fresh white T-shirt he wore underneath it. He took out his iPhone, opened Snapchat, and went to Vielle's Story.

There were numerous video clips. Vielle and her family were throwing a welcome home celebration for Hard. The whole house was alive with smiles and laughter. Trey had seen prison yard photos of Hard on Vee's social media, but it was different seeing him without the standard khakis and plain gray sweats. Hard was already kingpin fresh in Amiri with an icy Cuban-link on his neck and a diamond watch on his wrist. Vee moved her camera close enough to see every glistening detail of the jewelry.

In another video clip Trey saw Vielle's brother, Lorde, and three more young black men who were around his age. All four of them had big black guns that they repeatedly flashed in front of the camera — a Micro Draco with a banana clip, two AR pistols, and several Glocks.

Lorde pointed his Micro Draco and a Glock with a 50-shot drum at the camera and rapped along to the Lil Durk song that was playing in the background: "... You ain't have yo' gun for dem, you better keep yo' gun for me, better keep yo' gun for Boonie, better keep yo' gun for Cee. Think I'm playin' then come and see, you gon' end up by dat tree..." He stopped rapping and got serious, showing his diamond-encrusted teeth in a menacing scowl. "On bro, I wish a nigga would try to spin on us. Muhfuckas know where we at. All you gotta do is pull up. Getcho shit swiss-cheesed, on Chief."

Trey scowled. "I could care less about her brother and the niggas he got with him," he said finally. "They all live on the west side of Chicago. They don't know shit about Michigan City, and I bet money they'll be gone in a day or two. As soon as they leave I'm pullin' up. Vee gotta pay for this shit. I ain't gon' kill her or nothin', but I'ma have my baby mama stomp that bitch. And her punk ass daddy bet' not say shit."

Thirty gave a reluctant nod. "So should I FaceTime this man or not?"

"Hell naw!" Trey snapped. He sat forward on the sofa and pushed his feet down into the blue and gray Nike Vapor Maxes he'd kicked off a few minutes ago. "What the fuck you need to call him for? That nigga daughter shot me, and you thinkin' about talkin' to him? The fuck kinda shit is that?"

"Bro, calm down."

"Nah, ain't no calm down. Fuck a calm down. I could've died out there in that parkin' lot. That's y'all problem, you niggas way too friendly. Watch this, though." Trey pocketed his phone and, using his left hand, drew the Glock from his hip. He stood up and turned to face Thirty and Big Block. "Watch what I do to this bitch and her brother. Y'all wanna act all scared and shit. I'ma show you how to deal with them Chicago niggas. Bet they won't send no more Snapchat threats."

Chapter 4

Hard's mother and her sister Vicky were identical twins, and they'd spent the vast majority of their seventy years dressing alike. Tonight they wore red turtleneck sweaters over black pants and gold hoop earrings that matched the rings on their wrinkled old fingers. Auntie Vicky's husband, Tommy Parker, had passed away from lung cancer two years before Hard went away, but Mama's husband, James Gaing Sr., was present for the welcome home party. He was an inch shorter than Hard, a tall, gaunt old man with a long face and a skin complexion that was as dark as wet mud. He and Mama cried when they hugged Hard. He somehow managed to keep it together, moving on to embrace Auntie Vicky's two daughters and her one son — Grace, Treasure, and Tom-Tom. Altogether the siblings had ten children, four of whom had accompanied them here from Chicago.

Lorde's daughter Journee was just one of the sticky-fingered rugrats who wrapped themselves around Hard's pantlegs. Flower had three kids, all boys, and they came at him all at once. He picked them up one by one to give them each their own personal moment with the grandpa they hardly knew.

Hard found himself equally happy to shake hands and slap shoulders with two of his old friends. Their names were Freddy and Tone Bone, and they'd been with him and Tom-Tom at the time when the Michigan City Police Department alleged that he'd walked into Donovan Taylor's garage near the corner of 8th Street and Grant Avenue and shot him twice in the face for allegedly having an affair with Dominique Smiley, Hard's then-girlfriend and HJ's mother.

It was a good motive, a true motive, but the fact remained that Hard had been fifty-some miles away in Chicago, serving two bricks of cocaine to an old classmate of his on California and Polk.

Freddy had a lot of gray in the peach fuzz around his mouth, and there were a couple of empty spaces in his grin where twenty years ago there had been teeth. He wore a black sweatshirt with a big square photo on the chest that depicted him standing between Hard and Tone Bone on the rear deck of a yacht. It was from a business trip they'd taken to Cancun in the summer of 2004.

Tone Bone had the same image on the front of his black sweater. He was almost as tall as Hard and had fat braided dreadlocks that reached way down to his waist. There were no vacancies in his two neat rows of pearly whites. His eyes were as hard and unyielding as the muscle he concealed beneath a few healthy layers of fat, but there were tears rippling along his lower eyelids. His two diamond tennis chains didn't have any pendants dangling from them and quite frankly they didn't need any. His Audemars Piguet was just as captivatingly icy as Hard's Rolex. Unlike Freddy, who'd gone straight following a four-year stint in federal prison, Tone Bone was still neck-deep in the dope game. He'd maintained his relationship with the Matamoros drug cartel in the years since Hard left the streets. He'd done five and a half years in the Feds, from early 2008 to the middle of 2013, for attempting to drive across the border into Mexico with over four hundred thousand dollars stashed in the trunk of his car, and he fell back into his old ways as soon as he was released. For years Tone Bone had been putting together packages of drugs and cell phones for prison guards to smuggle in to Hard, and he rarely ever asked for payment.

Tone's huge black arms enveloped Hard in a bear hug that sapped all the breath from his lungs, and for the second time in less than five hours Hard found himself consoling a teary-eyed friend. Ironically, it was Hard's attempt to console Tone that kept him from shedding any tears himself.

"They done freed my mothafuckin' nigga!" Tone exclaimed, before turning to Vicky and Mama to apologize for his foul choice of words.

It was straight to the dining room after that. The cherrywood table was lined from end to end with aluminum pans of piping-hot soul food. Candy fixed two plates for Hard — a sixteen-ounce sirloin steak, Auntie Vicky's flavorful turkey-based greens, Mama's Velveeta-drenched spaghetti, two barbecue chicken breasts, and a fat chunk of cornbread.

Hard aye like a starved man. He'd purposely gone without eating his last day in prison so his appetite was nearly bottomless. He took big bites from the sirloin and crammed in huge forkfuls of cheesy spaghetti behind it. He sat at the head of the table, the "King of the Gaings," listening to the music of his family's chaos.

"Daddy, you remember when you called me for my sixteenth birthday and told me you had sent a 'package' to the house?" Vielle asked, leaning her chin on her hand, her hazel eye sparkling. "I thought it was gon' be a coat or some shoes. I opened that box and ten thousand dollars in fifties and twenties fell out on the floor. My boyfriend almost had a heart attack!"

The table erupted in laughter. Hard grinned, his teeth white against his groomed beard. "I had to make sure my baby girl was straight. I couldn't be there to take you to the mall, but I could damn sure make sure the mall came to you."

"And he did the same for me," Flower added, wiping a smudge of grease from her youngest son's face. "Every graduation, every prom. You was there in the pockets, even if you wasn't there in the pictures. Everybody thought we was rich."

Hard felt a lump in his throat that had nothing to do with the steak. He looked at Lorde, who was seated with his daughter on his lap, watching her laugh as he kissed the palms of her little hands. He looked at his mother, whose face seemed to have found peace for the first time in two decades. But his gaze kept drifting back to Candy.

She was sitting close, her thigh pressed against his. Every time he laughed, her hand found his bicep. The scent of her perfume—something floral and expensive—was cutting through the heavy aroma of soul food, and it was driving him crazy. Twenty years of cold steel and industrial disinfectant had made him crave the softness of a woman like a man dying of thirst.

He leaned in close to her ear, his voice a low, gravelly vibration. "I appreciate the party, baby. I really do. But if I don't get you alone in the next five minutes, I might just pass out from the tension."

Candy's lips curled into a knowing, sultry smile. She stood up, smoothing down her skintight jeans. "Excuse us for a minute, y'all. I gotta show Hard where I put his... extra luggage upstairs."

A chorus of catcalls and "Oooohs" followed them as they left the room. Lorde gave a knowing grin and nodded his approval.

"Don't be up there too long!" Lorde shouted, flashing his diamond grill. "The ribs ain't even out the oven yet!"

"Mind your business!" Hard called back over his shoulder, not looking back.

The stairs creaked under his weight—a solid, real sound of a real home. When they reached the landing, Candy led him into the master bedroom. It was a sanctuary of deep greys and navys, with a king-sized bed that looked like a cloud compared to the thin, plastic-covered mat he'd occupied for two decades at ISP.

The moment the door clicked shut, the world outside—the threats from Trey, the noise of the party, the shadow of the prison—vanished.

Hard grabbed Candy by the waist, lifting her off her feet as his mouth found hers. It wasn't a gentle kiss; it was a desperate, hungry mashing of lips. He pressed her back against the door, his large hands roaming the curves he'd only been allowed to imagine through a glass partition or a brief, monitored hug in a visiting room.

"You have no idea," he groaned against her neck, his breath hot, "how many nights I spent staring at a concrete ceiling, just trying to imagine exactly how you felt."

Candy wrapped her legs around his waist, her fingers digging into the soft fabric of his Amiri hoodie. "You don't have to imagine no more, bae. I'm right here. And I ain't going nowhere."

Hardly any words were spoken after that. Hard locked the door. Candy undressed herself first, slowly and seductively, and then she took her sweet time stripping her man down to his boxer briefs.

"Yes," she said, moving to her knees in front of him and caressing his growing erection through the fabric of his underwear. She kissed him on the stomach, an inch to the left of his belly button, and then she peeled his briefs all the way down to his ankles and planted a second smooch on the head of his dick.

Taking his thick erection in both hands, she stroked it and spit on it and opened her mouth to stuff it down her throat. Hard was incredibly well-endowed — eleven and a half inches of girthy dark meat — and he was genuinely surprised at how much of it she was able to make disappear.

For several blissful minutes he stood there looking down at her with his mouth hanging open and his eyelids fluttering. She sucked him good and deep. It wasn't long before his entire length was covered in her bubbly saliva. She smacked herself across the face with it, squeezed and stroked it. She massaged and sucked on his balls.

"Oh, shit," he said, three or four times in a row.

She took him out of her mouth, smacked herself on the jaw with his glistening wet shaft, and then took him back into her throat.

Hard didn't want to ejaculate prematurely but it happened just the same. Candy sensed it coming and tilted her head back with her mouth wide open for the cumshot. Hot white ropes of semen splashed onto the flat of her extended tongue, and she swallowed greedily.

"Mmm," she moaned, squeezing and stroking him until every last drop was on her tongue. She licked her lips and smiled up at him. "That was fast, Hard. I mean, I know it's been a while, but damn. You couldn't last five minutes?"

Hard laughed and fell back onto the bed. He stared at the ceiling, just breathing and smiling. Candy climbed on top of him and sat down on his softening magic stick.

"Just give me a minute," he said, rubbing her thigh. "Damn. You didn't tell me you was low-key Superhead."

Biting her bottom lip, Candy rolled off of him and lay there next to him with her legs cocked open, using her fingers to rub and massage her unattended lady parts. She slipped two fingers inside and they came out slippery. Soon the delicious scent of her sex filled the air, and Hard had no choice but to return the favor.

He moved onto his stomach like a sniper and began flickering his tongue between the meaty folds of her pussy...

Chapter 5

The heavy, thumping bass of King Von's "War With Us" rattled the interior panels of the matte black Suburban as it crept into the mouth of the alley. The vehicle moved like a predator in tall grass, its headlights killed, relying only on the dim glow of the moon reflecting off the icy slush. The air inside was thick and hazy. A blunt of "Moonrock" moved between Thirty's fat fingers, the scent of the exotic strain—pungent, skunky, and chemically sweet—clinging to the leather upholstery.

Thirty took a long, deep pull, the cherry glowing bright orange in the dark. He exhaled a cloud of smoke that obscured the rearview mirror before passing it back to Trey. The Glock pistol on his lap had a silver button behind the slide and a 50-shot drum beneath the butt.

"I'm tellin' you, li'l bro, this move is sloppy," Thirty said, his voice straining to be heard over Von's aggressive flow. He looked at the back of the burgundy house. Lights were on in the kitchen and one upstairs window. "Hard just touched down. The whole family in there. We shoot that crib up tonight, you ain't just hittin' Vee. You hittin' innocent family members, you hittin' kids. You checkin' us into a war we might not win."

Trey took the blunt with his left hand, his right shoulder screaming in protest even through the fog of the Percocets. He didn't look at his brother. His eyes were fixed on the back door of the house—the door to the enclosed porch.

"I don't give a fuck who in there," Trey rasped, his voice cold and heartless. "She put a bullet in me. My blood is on that parking lot concrete because of her. You worried about 'the bag,' Thirty. I'm worried about my respect. If I let a bitch pop me and I don't do nothin', I'm dead in the streets anyway. Ain't nobody gon' respect me."

Big Block sat in the back, his massive frame hunched forward, eyes scanning the alleyway. "Thirty right about one thing," Block rumbled. "That gray Trackhawk out front? That's Lorde's. Them TVL niggas don't play. They'll have this whole block lookin' like a war zone if they run out here shootin'."

"Then let it be a war zone," Trey snapped.

He handed the blunt back to Thirty and reached into his waistband. He pulled the Glock 22—the very gift Vielle had bought him—and felt the cold weight of the 22-shot extended magazine. The irony wasn't lost on him; he was going to use her own love to tear her world apart.

Trey pressed the button on the door panel. The window slid down with a faint, mechanical hiss, letting in a sudden, sharp blast of winter air. The snow swirled into the cabin, mixing with the marijuana smoke.

Thirty grabbed Trey's forearm. "Trey, don't. Think about the play, man. Think about the money. I done made damn near half a million fuckin' with Vee's brother. Got a whole house built from the ground up. We can walk in there and make peace, folks. On David. We can walk in there and talk to these niggas like men."

Trey shook him off with a violent jerk. "Think about this."

He leaned toward the open window, the cold air biting at his face. He extended his right arm, bracing the Glock against the door frame. The house looked peaceful, the muffled sound of Al Green drifting faintly from the front of the building, completely unaware of the shadow in the alley.

Trey squinted, his finger tightening on the trigger, the iron sights centered right on the glowing window where the light was brightest.

Chapter 6

The celebration inside the burgundy house didn't just end; it was vaporized.

One moment, Al Green was crooning about happiness, and the next, the sharp, rhythmic clack-clack-clack of a Glock 22 tore through the night air. Trey squeezed the trigger with a vengeful rhythm, the muzzle flashes illuminating the interior of the Suburban like a strobe light.

But he wasn't the only one with a gun out.

Baby Lord had been standing on the back porch, leaning against an old ten-speed Huffy to catch a breath of cold air and check his phone. He was a dark-skinned kid with deep, 360-waves and a bright future in Lorde's circle. He just so happened to have his gun in his hand. As soon as the shooting started he dropped his phone and shot back, throwing open the door and rushing out onto the steps, but he was only able to let off a couple of shots. One of Trey's opening rounds caught him squarely in the right eyebrow. His head snapped back, and he collapsed onto the snow-covered porch steps without a sound, his life ending before his body hit the wood.

"Shoot back! Shoot back! Blow dem niggas down!" Lorde roared from the kitchen, diving over the granite island. He didn't panic; he reacted. He snatched his Micro Draco from the counter, the banana clip rattling as he slid the bolt back.

The back window exploded inward. Flower, reaching for her middle son, let out a piercing scream as a stray round tore through the palm of her hand, shattering the delicate bones. Blood sprayed across the "Welcome Home" banner. Several more rounds popped a bunch of balloons and splintered the kitchen cabinets.

But the real tragedy happened in the center of the room. Journee, clutching a half-eaten chicken drumstick, had been running toward the kitchen to find her dad. A .40-caliber round punched through the clapboard siding of the house and caught the five-year-old high in the chest. The force threw her small frame backward onto the rug.

Lorde didn't see his daughter fall; he was too busy returning fire. He swung the back door open and unleashed the Draco. The thunderous thump-thump-thump of 7.62 rounds dwarfed Trey's handgun. He took aim at the idling SUV, immediately recognizing it as Thirty's truck.

Lil Luke and Fayzo flanked the doorway, their AR pistols spitting fire into the alley. The Suburban's windshield turned into a spider web of cracks. It's side windows shattered.

"Go! Drive, nigga,. DRIVE!" Trey screamed, ducking in his seat as rifle rounds began to chew through the Suburban's heavy doors.

Thirty didn't need to be told twice. He slammed the SUV into reverse, the tires screaming against the slushy gravel. In the backseat, Big Block let out a guttural groan. Two rifle rounds had pierced the rear door—one catching him in the meaty part of his shoulder and another tearing through his thigh.

"I'm hit! Thirty, I'm hit!" Block yelled, his wine-barrel voice cracking with pain.

Thirty stomped the gas, fishtailing the massive SUV out of the narrow alley. The vehicle looked like Swiss cheese, coolant leaking from the radiator and the passenger-side mirror hanging by a wire. As they sped away, Lorde looked back and saw that a bullet had caught Tom-Tom in the side of the stomach. He went down hard, clutching his midsection, but his breath was still coming in ragged, painful gasps.

Inside, the music had stopped. The only sound was the high-pitched ringing in everyone's ears and the sound of sobbing.

Hard and Candy came thundering down the stairs, Hard's face a mask of pure, ancestral fury. He reached the bottom step just as Lorde was dropping his Draco, his eyes wide and fixed on the floor.

"Journee?" Lorde whispered, his voice breaking.

Hard pushed past him, his heart stopping. He saw his granddaughter lying on the rug, the bright red of her blood staining the white "Amiri"lettering on his own chest as he scooped her up. Her eyes were fluttering, her breath coming in tiny, wet hitches.

"No, no, no," Hard growled, his voice a terrifying vibration. "Not like this. Journee, look at Papi. Look at me!"

But the light in her eyes was fading. Beside her, Flower was cradling her shattered hand, and Tom-Tom was being dragged into the hallway by Tone Bone to stem the bleeding. Baby Lord lay dead on the porch, the snow around his head turning a deep, dark crimson.

Hardis Gaing Sr. looked up from his dying granddaughter's face. The "Love, Truth, Peace"he'd talked about earlier was gone. In its place was the cold-blooded monster that had ruled Chicago's West Side streets twenty years ago.

He looked at Lorde, who was staring at his daughter's blood on his own hands.

"Get the guns," Hard said, his voice deathly quiet. "Every last one of 'em. We ain't waiting for the police."

Chapter 7

The sirens cut through the freezing night, a discordant symphony of grief and authority. Blue and red strobes bounced off the blood-stained snow in the driveway, turning the crime scene into a flickering nightmare.

Hard sat on the porch steps, his Moncler coat open, his brand-new Amiri hoodie ruined by the dark, drying stains of his granddaughter's lifeblood. He didn't move. He didn't blink. He just stared left and right, unconsciously keeping an eye on each corner in case the shooters returned.

A royal blue Ford Explorer screeched to a halt at the curb. HJ vaulted out of the driver's seat before the engine had even fully died. He wasn't the detective now; he was a son and a brother running toward a house that felt like a tomb. He pushed past a patrol officer trying to tape off the perimeter.

"Move!" HJ barked, flashing his gold badge with a shaking hand.

He hit the porch and stopped dead. He saw Baby Lord being zipped into a black bag by the coroner's crew. Then his eyes moved to the living room.

Several EMTs were moving with practiced, frantic speed. They had Tom-Tom on a gurney, a pressure bandage taped over the jagged hole in his abdomen. He was pale, his eyes rolling back, but he was breathing. Behind him, Flower was being led to a second ambulance, her hand wrapped in a thick bulb of white gauze that was rapidly turning red. She was hysterical, her screams for Journee muffled by the oxygen mask they were trying to fit over her face.

"Where is she?" HJ demanded, his voice cracking as he looked at Hard. "Pops, where is Journee?"

Hard didn't answer. He just tilted his head toward the interior of the house.

HJ stepped inside and saw Lorde. His younger brother was on his knees in the center of the rug, his forehead pressed against the floor. He wasn't crying—he was making a low, rhythmic keening sound, like a wounded animal. The Micro Draco lay three feet away, cold and empty. Lorde's designer clothes were smeared with the same crimson that marked their father.

"Lorde..." HJ started, reaching out.

"Don't touch me!" Lorde screamed, snapping his head up. His eyes were bloodshot, his diamond grill bared in a snarl of pure agony. "My daughter dead, nigga! She dead! Them niggas killed my baby!"

A veteran sergeant named Richard Miller stepped out of the kitchen, flipping his notebook shut. He looked at HJ, then at the heavy artillery sitting on the granite countertops—the AR pistols and the Glocks that Lorde's boys hadn't even bothered to hide.

"We checked the neighbor's Ring cam," Miller said quietly to HJ. "Black Suburban crept through the alley. They fired first. Your brother and his associates... they were just protecting the home. Couldn't get them to give a statement, butit's a clean case of self-defense, Gaing. We're recovering .40-caliber casings from the alley. Your people's brass is all inside the house and on the back porch. We aren't taking anyone in tonight. Not from here, at least."

The police were backing off, leaving the family to grieve. They knew what this was. They knew that arresting Hardis Gaing on his first night home simply because he was present during the shooting wouldn't hold up in court—and it might just start a dispute they weren't ready to handle.

The house was too loud with the silence of the dead. Grace and Treasure emerged from the back bedroom, their faces tear-streaked but set with purpose. They had Mama and Auntie Vicky by the arms. The two older women looked fragile, their red turtleneck sweaters suddenly looking like shrouds. Mama stopped to pat and squeeze Hard's shoulder, the reassuring squeeze she'd always given him when times got tough.

"We're taking them to your mom's house on Barker Avenue," Grace whispered as she passed Hard on the porch. "They can't stay here. Not with the blood. Not with all the bullet holes."

Hard finally stood up. He watched as they loaded his mother into the car to head to the East Side. He waited until the taillights disappeared into the fog of an incipient snowstorm.

He turned to HJ, who was standing in the doorway, caught between the law he represented and the blood he came from.

"You're a detective, son," Hard said, his voice as cold as the ice under his boots. "So detect. You find out exactly who did this and let me know. You find out where that Suburban went, and don't report the shit to your so-called superiors. Let me keep this shit in the streets."

"Pops, you gotta let me handle this the right way," HJ pleaded. "Ain't no sense in you risking your freedom after twenty years in prison. Come on, now, you're smarter than that. I know you are."

Hard stepped into his son's space, his 6'5" frame towering over the detective. "The 'right way' died on that rug tonight. You ain't got a niece no more. Lorde ain't got a daughter. Some chump just dumped a whole clip into my house before I could even get comfortable enough to call it a home, and I'll be god-damned if I don't do some'n about it. Now, are you gonna be a Gaing, or are you gonna be a witness?"2 the zaaq as@@@

Chapter 8

The Percocets weren't doing the job anymore. The adrenaline had worn off, leaving Trey gripped by a crippling, white-hot pain in his shoulder, but it was nothing compared to the sounds coming from the backseat. Big Block was fading, his deep voice reduced to a wet, bubbly wheeze as his life leaked out onto the Suburban's leather.

"Bruh, he bleedin' out! Drop him off! We gotta hurry up and drop this nigga off!" Trey barked, clutching his Glock with a tight-knuckled grip.

Thirty's eyes were huge in their sockets. He swung the bullet-battered SUV into the ambulance bay of the emergency room, the tires screeching against the concrete. They didn't park. Thirty hopped out, yanked the rear door open, and practically rolled Big Block's massive, limp frame onto the pavement right in front of the sliding glass doors. Two older black women who were standing there smoking gasped in horror. Thirty recognized one of them as the mother of an aspiring young hustler to whom he'd recently sold eight pounds of White Runtz.

"Good luck, Block," Thirty muttered, his heart hammering against his ribs. He didn't have the time to wait for a nurse; he saw one, a slim, bespectacled white woman sitting behind the desk inside the waiting room, but he didn't wave for her. He jumped back into the driver's seat and floored it, the Suburban's dragging muffler sparking against the ground as they fled into the night.

They headed deep into the East Side, weaving through narrow residential streets until they found a desolate alleyway clogged with unplowed snow and overflowing trash bins. Thirty killed the engine, and the silence that followed was deafening. The Suburban was a graveyard of broken glass and spent shell casings. There was a song playing from the speakers — "Break the Bank" by Bulletface and Young Meach — but the sound was low and distorted, and Thirty knew that meant his two 15-inch speakers were blown.

"Call Tyrisha," Thirty ordered, wiping sweat from his forehead. "Now. Before the GPS on this bitch leads the law right to us."

Trey fumbled with his phone, his breath coming in ragged gasps. Tyrisha Tanner was the only play they had left. At thirty-one, she was a high-achieving orthopedic surgeon with a penchant for "bad boys" that her medical board colleagues would never understand.

"Reesh? It's me. I need you. East side, 9th Street, the alley behind the liquor store. Come in the truck. Hurry up, big baby. Please."

Ten minutes later, a bubblegum-pink Cadillac Escalade turned into the alley, its LED headlights cutting through the falling snow. Tyrisha sat behind the wheel, her scrubs still on under a designer fur coat. She was a heavy-set woman with a sharp mind for bone density and a blind spot for Treykwan Murray.

"Trey! Oh my God, you're bleeding!" she shrieked as they scrambled toward the Caddy.

"Just drive, Reesh! Just get us outta here!" Trey scrambled into the passenger seat, while Thirty dove into the back, his eyes darting around the dark alley.

They hadn't even closed the doors when a pair of headlights rounded the corner of the alley, blinding them. The engine roar was unmistakable—the high-pitched whine of a BMW M-series.

"Is that...?" Thirty started, his voice trailing off in horror.

Vielle.

She wasn't crying anymore. Her face was a mask of cold, hazel-eyed vengeance as she leaned out of the driver's side window of her jet-black coupe. No words were shouted. She didn't warn them. She simply raised her .45-caliber Springfield and let the lead fly.

POW! POW-POW-POW!

The first round caught the Escalade's rear passenger window, turning the expensive glass into a million diamonds that rained down on Thirty. Another round thudded into the Cadillac's heavy door.

"AHHHHHH!" Tyrisha screamed, a sound of pure, unadulterated terror. She ducked her head, screamed again, and then she slammed the Escalade into gear and floored it, the massive SUV roaring as it bumped over a trashcan and took the corner post off a backyard chain link fence.

"She's following us! Trey, she's still on us!" Thirty yelled, looking back to see the BMW's headlights stuck to their bumper like a shadow.

Tyrisha's professional composure had vanished. She was sobbing, her hands shaking so hard the Escalade was swerving across both lanes. "I can't do this! I'm a doctor! I'm a doctor!"

"Turn here! Get us to the highway!" Trey yelled, but Tyrisha wasn't listening to him anymore. She saw the lights in the windows of the Michigan City Police Department headquarters glowing a few blocks ahead. It was the only place she felt safe.

She veered the pink Escalade across three lanes of traffic, tires screaming, and headed straight for the MCPD parking lot with Vielle's BMW hot on her heels, the gun sticking out the driver's window still spitting fire into the cold winter night.

Chapter 9

Gritting her teeth, Vielle watched the pink Escalade swerve violently into the brightly lit parking lot of the Michigan City Police Department. For a split second, the green laser of her Springfield danced across the Cadillac's liftgate, but the sight of a blue-and-white cruiser pulling out from the side of the building snapped her back to reality.

"Fuck!" she hissed, tucking the gun into her waistband and yanking the steering wheel to the right.

There was no sense in waiting for the sirens to find her. She hammered the gas, the BMW's engine roaring as she tore down Michigan Boulevard. Her heart was a frantic drum in her chest, the image of Journee's small, limp body on the rug burned into her retinas. She took the turn onto 8th Street at a dangerous clip, the back end of the coupe fishtailing through the slush before the tires bit and propelled her west.

She drove like a woman possessed, blowing through the stop sign at Grant Avenue—right past the area where her daddy had been wrongfully accused twenty years ago. She didn't stop until she saw the familiar porch light at 8th and Green.

Vielle didn't knock. She threw the door open and stumbled into the warmth of Bambi's house, her breath coming in ragged, freezing gasps.

The vibe inside was a world away from the carnage on 7th Street. The air was thick with the chemical tang of crystal meth and the heavy bass of a slow R&B track. Bambi was perched comfortably on the lap of Victor "Baby Gang"

Lewis, her arms draped around his neck. Baby Gang looked exactly like his pictures—dark, sharp-featured, and undeniably fine. He was tall, maybe six-three, and all of his teeth were sheathed in gold. The tattoo across the front of his neck read "Money Gang" in slanted slime lettering. On the coffee table in front of them, Shaggy and Meko were hunched over a digital scale, their fingers moving with clinical precision as they bagged up translucent shards of meth.

"Vee? Bitch, what the hell?" Bambi started, her eyes widening as she took in Vielle's disheveled state.

Vielle hardly even acknowledged the men. She marched over, grabbed Bambi by the wrist with a grip like iron, and hauled her off Baby Gang's lap.

"I need you. Now," Vielle said.

"Whoa, watch the hands, lil mama," Meko muttered, looking up from the scale, but one look at the hollow, murderous expression in Vielle's hazel eye made him rethink his tone.

Vielle dragged Bambi into the back bedroom and slammed the door shut, leaning her back against it. The tears finally came, hot and blurring. Her chest hitched. She sniffled, wiped her nose, and shook her head despondently.

"They came to the house, Bambi," Vielle sobbed, the words tumbling out in a rush. "Trey and Thirty. They sprayed the whole crib. Journee... she's gone, sis. They killed my niece. They shot Flower, they shot my cousin Tom-Tom... it was a bloodbath. My daddy just got home a few hours ago and he had to hold that baby while she died. My brother was there, and he had to watch his baby take her last breath."

Bambi's mouth fell open, her hand flying to her chest. "Oh my God, Vee... Journee? No... not that sweet little baby."

Vielle spent the next ten minutes shaking and crying, recounting the shooting at her 7th Street home and the chase with the pink Escalade. She hopes to God she'd hit Trey or

Thirty with a bullet or two. She was vibrating with a mix of grief and unspent adrenaline.

Bambi waited for the initial wave of hysteria to pass, rubbing Vielle's shoulders. But as Vielle's breathing slowed, Bambi's expression shifted. She looked back toward the door, then back at Vielle, a strange, opportunistic glint in her eyes.

"Listen to me, Vee," Bambi whispered, leaning in close. "You're crashing. You're gonna end up back at that police station or in a grave if you don't calm your nerves. You need to get your mind off the drama for a second."

"How? How am I supposed to do that? Some niggas just shot up my whole mother fuckin' house. I just watched my niece take her last breath. How in the fuck am I supposed to calm down after some shit like that?"

Bambi chewed her lip, a sultry smile tugging at her full mouth. "Baby Gang is out there. He's been asking about you ever since we talked about you liking his pictures. He likes that 'pretty-eyed savage' energy you got going on; his words, not mine. Why don't you come out there? Me, you, and him. We can get high, get lost in each other, and just let the world disappear for a few hours. A little 'us' time to take the edge off. What you think? You know he's the finest nigga on the West Side."

Vielle stared at her best friend, the grief in her chest feeling like a heavy stone. Out in the living room, she could hear the clinking of the glass shards and the low rumble of Baby Gang's laugh. Her hands wouldn't stop trembling. She'd suspected for months that Trey had been cheating on her with Tyrisha, and now that she'd shot up Tyrisha's truck she felt a whole lot better about it. Now it was her turn to fuck somebody else, and who better than the man she'd gotten into it with Trey over to begin with?

"Man, fuck it," Vee said, after a time. "Fuck it, let's do it. I don't wanna go back outside anyway. It's too much going on, and if I have to go back home and see the spot where my niece got killed I might just end up shooting myself."

With a defeated sigh and a desolate head shake, she let Bambi lead her back out to the living room.

The heavy, sweet scent of three Moonrock blunts acted like a chemical curtain, shielding Vielle from the raw, razor-sharp edges of the reality waiting for her back on 7th Street. She sat on the edge of Bambi's velvet sofa, her lungs burning with the thick, expensive smoke as she exhaled a cloud that hung in the air like a ghost.

Beside her, Baby Gang was a constant, grounding presence. He was dark and smooth, his movements languid as he leaned back, one arm draped over the top of the sofa behind Vielle's head. He was smooth enough to know that he didn't need to push; he just sat there, smiling and talking about sports and street shit with his boys, an apex predator waiting for the storm to subside so he could strike. Shaggy and Meko had finished bagging the meth and were now focused on the blunts, the orange cherries glowing like tiny signals in the hazy dimness of the room. Meko — a brown-skinned, stocky young man with long dreads that were tied up in a messy pile on top of his round head — had a thick stack of wrinkled cash in one hand and a weed-stuffed Backwoods cigar wedges between the fingers of the other. He had on a royal blue Nike Tech outfit with matching Jordans. Shaggy was taller, slimmer, and he too was wearing a Nike Tech outfitonly his was black and his shoes were clean black Nike Vapor Maxes.

Vielle's world, however, was condensed into the six-inch screen of her iPhone 17. Her thumb moved with an obsessive rhythm, scrolling through Facebook and Snapchat.

The Michigan City "word of mouth" was moving faster than the police scanners.

She checked her Facebook page and read the most recent post a man named Marcus Butler had shared from the MCPD page: Multiple shootings reported overnight. One fatality confirmed, a juvenile. Police on scene at 7th St and Willard Ave.

One comment from a woman named Muriel Shoemaker read: 'I heard it was Hardis Gaing's people. Nigga just got out tonight and the city already on fire. Rest in peace to that baby girl.'

Another comment from a woman named Tequila Hammond read: 'They say it was Vielle who shot Trey the other night. He caught her cheating on him with Baby Gang and they got to fighting. Ion know how true it is but that's what I heard.'

On Snapchat she saw that Trey had posted: "Krazy when the ppl you love and do anything for turn on you. Shot by the person you gave your heart to. Shit wild, on David."

Vielle felt a surge of bile in her throat when she saw Trey's post. He was playing the victim, acting like he hadn't beat on her and choked her and then gone on to empty a clip into a house full of women and children. She wanted to scream, to run back out to her BMW and hunt them down until her Springfield clicked empty, but the weed was pulling her down into the cushions, making her limbs feel like lead.

"Put that phone down, Vee," Bambi said, sliding a fresh blunt into Vielle's hand. "Social media ain't gonna bring her back, and it sure as hell ain't gonna keep you out of handcuffs. Look at me. Look at us."

Vielle looked up just as the front door burst open. Tonya and Kela drifted in like a pair of high-fashion video vixens. Tonya was light-skinned with a waist-length weave and curves that defied physics; Kela was a deep chocolate brown, her eyes hooded and mischievous, carrying two chilled bottles of Hennessy like they were trophies.

"The party has arrived!" Kela announced, slamming the bottles onto the coffee table right next to the digital scales. "We heard the city was hot, so we decided to bring the fire over here."

"Turn that shit up!" Tonya shouted, pointing toward the Bluetooth speaker.

The smooth R&B was abruptly cut off by the raucous, aggressive energy of Sexyy Redd. The bass was so heavy it made the glass on the coffee table vibrate.

"Shake yo dreads, shake yo dreads..."

The atmosphere in the room shifted instantly. The trauma of the evening was pushed into the corner as the liquor started flowing. Paper cups were filled to the rim with Hennessy, and the girls began to move. Tonya and Kela didn't need an invitation; they were already in the center of the rug, their bodies moving like pole dancers at Magic City.

Bambi stood up, her caramel skin glowing under the dim lights as she joined them. She looked back at Vielle, beckoning her with a flick of her wrist. "Come on, Vee! Let it go! Just for tonight, bitch! Turn up!"

Vielle watched them. She watched the way Tonya's hips swayed and the way Kela dropped low, her hands on her knees, shaking her ass for Shaggy and Meko, who were cheering and recording the scene on their phones. Baby Gang's hand finally moved, his fingers grazing the back of Vielle's neck, sending a shiver down her spine that had nothing to do with the cold.

"You too pretty to be this sad, lil mama," Baby Gang whispered over the music. "Let me see what you working with. Bounce that ass for a real nigga."

Vielle took a long, burning swallow of the Hennessy. The alcohol hit her stomach like a lightning bolt, finally snapping the last thread of her restraint. She stood up, but the smell of the gunpowder and the faint, copper scent of Journee's blood on her shirt made her pause.

"I need to wash this off me," Vielle muttered.

Bambi was on her in a second, leading her toward the bathroom. "I got you, sis. Take a shower. Scrub it all away. I'll leave some clothes out for you."

The hot water was a mercy. Vielle stood under the spray for twenty minutes, scrubbing her skin until it was red, trying to wash away the memory of her bloody kitchen and the feel of the gun recoiling in her hand. When she stepped out, she found a small, white cropped tee and a pair of black spandex booty shorts that Bambi had left on the counter.

She dressed quickly, looking at herself in the mirror. Her smoky gray dead eye looked more haunting than ever against her flushed skin. She looked like a ghost that had decided to haunt a party.

When she walked back into the living room, the vibe had reached a fever pitch. The room was a haze of smoke and Hennessy. Two more girls — Tiana Cooper and Jayla Sutton — had joined the party. Tonya and Kela were practically on the floor, twerking to the beat while Meko threw a handful of one-dollar bills over them.

Bambi was leaning against the wall, watching Vielle. As Vielle approached, Bambi reached out, hooking her fingers into the waistband of Vielle's shorts and pulling her close. The scent of alcohol was heavy on her breath.

"There she go," Bambi murmured. "There go my bitch."

Without warning, Bambi leaned in. The kiss was slow, tasting of weed and cognac, a soft collision of feminine lips that finally blurred the edges of Vielle's consciousness. Vielle wanted to pull away but didn't. She leaned into the warmth, needing to feel anything other than the cold vacuum of grief. It wasn't like this was her first time kissing a girl; back in Houston, she'd actually dated a girl for a little over a year. She'd hated it in the end, but there had definitely been some good times. Some good orgasms, too.

Baby Gang stood up from the sofa. He didn't say a word as he walked over to them, his dark eyes fixed on the two shorter women. All four of his canine teeth were coated with gold and diamonds, while the rest of his teeth were plain gold. He reached out, his large hands finding the small of their backs, and began to guide them toward the bedroom.

"Shaggy, Meko," Baby Gang called over his shoulder, his voice low and commanding. "Y'all keep the party going out here. Don't nobody knock on this door unless the feds on the porch."

The bedroom door clicked shut, sealing out the Sexyy Redd track and the shouts of the party. The silence in the room was heavy, broken only by the sound of their breathing.

Vielle felt Baby Gang's hands on her, kneading the meat of her buttocks like dough, pulling her and Bambi toward the large, unmade bed. For the first time in hours, her mind wasn't on the Springfield .45 in her purse or the abusive ex she'd shot through the shoulder. It wasn't on Thirty's unbothered glance or the way Journee's eyes had gone dark in her final seconds.

She was drowning in the heat of the moment, a hollow, desperate escape that she knew would haunt her when the sun came up. But for now, in the darkness of Bambi's neatly furnished bedroom, the war was on the other side of the door.

"You don't know how long I been on yo' big-booty ass," Baby Gang said, licking his lips and staring at Vee as he fell back into the bed. "That nigga Meko, too. He was with me when we saw you at the club a few months ago. You had on that tight red Fendi dress. That ass was so muhfuckin' fat."

Bambi giggled. "Baby Gang, will you stand up?" And when he obliged she promptly yanked his pants down to his ankles and kneeled in front of him, running her fingertips along the impressive length of meat in his black and gold Calvin Klein boxer briefs.

Vielle spent a cautious couple of seconds eyeing the Glock pistol he had secured in a brown leather holster under his left arm. Then her eyes dropped to his crotch as Bambi peeled down his briefs and let his dick boing free.

"Take that shit off," he said, and lifted the front of Vee's cropped shirt.

He didn't have to ask her twice. The weed and liquor had set Vielle's loins ablaze. She and Bambi stripped themselves and then teamed up to strip their man. He laid back on the bed and smiled like a boss while the two girls positioned themselves on their hands and knees on either side of him.

"Hell yeah," he said emphatically. He smacked Vielle on the ass and watched as she and Bambi began kissing all over his erection. "My birthday in February, but I'm celebrating that muhfucka right now. On Vice Lord."

Hearing him swear on Vice Lord made Vee's chest swell with pride. Her father was a notorious leader of the Traveler Vice Lords. He loved the gang so much that he'd named his daughters Vielle (VL) and Flower, which was what you called a female Vice Lord, and he'd named one of his boys Lorde. Vee didn't know much about the hierarchical structure of the gang, but she knew that her daddy was a real high-ranker in the organization, and that he was often referred to as a 'chief' or a 'UE.' Knowing that Baby Gang and Hard were essentially on the same team made her smile for the first time since the shooting.

Vee closed her lips around the head of his dick while Bambi sucked on his clean-shaven balls. Bobbing her head, Vee stared over into Baby Gang's eyes. She watched his Adam's apple rise and fall like a monkey on a stick as he tipped his head back to gaze emptily at the ceiling.

"Hell yeah," he repeated.

Vee smiled around his dick and then went bananas, spitting and slurping and stroking it and then handing it over to Bambi so her friend could do the same thing. After that Bambi took a condom out of the brown paper bag on her nightstand. Baby Gang put it on himself.

"Can I fuck both of y'all with the same condom, or ..."

Bambi said "Yeah" and Vielle said "No" in the same instant. Which made Bambi frown and give Vee a quizzical side eye.

"I don't wanna offset my pH balance," Vee explained.

Baby Gang chuckled and said nothing. He kneeled behind Vielle, ran his hands across the fat mounds of her ass, and slowly guided his girthy phallus into her snug, slippery vaginal canal.

The man knew what he was doing back there. Clap-clap-clap-clap went the sound of his skin against hers. He smacked her on the ass every couple of strokes.

She knew that the view from his vantage point was stunning. She had the kind of body most strippers paid thousands of dollars for, a fat ghetto booty and thick thighs below a small waist, a nicely toned stomach, and big perky titties that bounced like balloons as Baby Gang pounded her out from the back.

She licked Bambi's pussy while BG dicked her down. It both tasted and smelled good, and she felt kind of bad about the whole condom dilemma, so she ate Bambi out like her pussy was the tastiest dessert on the menu.

It was most certainly a night to remember.

Chapter 10

The sun hadn't even fully cleared the horizon over Lake Michigan, but the light filtering through the blinds of the master bedroom felt like an interrogation lamp to Hard. He lay flat on his back, staring at the ceiling fan's slow rotation. Beside him, Candy was a soft, rhythmic presence, her breathing deep and untroubled—the only peace left in the bullet-riddled house.

Every time Hard closed his eyes, he didn't see the woman he loved or the life he'd dreamed of for twenty years. He saw the gold "Amiri" logo on his chest turning dark with Journee's blood. He saw the light leaving her hazel eyes. He saw Flower's bloodied hand, and Tom-Tom's bleeding stomach.

He slid out from under the silk sheets with the silence of a ghost, his massive frame barely making the floorboards creak. He grabbed his phone and retreated into the bathroom, clicking the door shut. He sat on the edge of the clawfoot tub and hit the contact for Millionaire Markio.

The video call connected almost instantly. The background wasn't a bedroom; it was the sleek, cream-leather interior of a Gulfstream G650.

Markio looked into the camera, looking every bit the mogul. He was short, handsome, and light-skinned, his 360-waves shimmering under the cabin lights. Even at this hour, he was draped in several diamond necklaces that caught the morning sun hitting the jet's windows. Flawless diamonds glittered on his perfect square teeth.

"Big Homie," Markio said, his voice smooth but laced with concern. "I been seeing the news. I was gon' call you as soon as we touched down in Teterboro. We got the screening for The Bird Man 3 tonight, but my heart is back there in MC with you. Anything you need, just ask. I got you."

Beside him, his fiancée, Morena, leaned into the frame. She was a stunning mulatto woman, her long, curly black hair cascading over her shoulders. Even sitting down, the sheer scale of her curves was evident as she shifted in the seat.

"We are so sorry, Hard," Morena said, her voice soft and genuine. "Journee was an angel. I was just looking at the pictures they posted of her on Instagram. She was so pretty."

"She was," Hard rasped, his voice sounding like it had been dragged over gravel. He gave them the grim rundown—the threats, the Suburban, the cowardice of Trey shooting into a house full of women and children.

Markio's expression hardened, the celebrity persona dropping to reveal the street-smart hustler who had helped Hard build an empire decades ago. He leaned forward, his diamonds clinking against his silk Louis Vuitton shirt. His forehead wrinkled. His eyes went asquint. His jaw muscles tightened.

"Listen to me, Hard. You're on papers. You can't be out here shopping for guns. I got some crates in a warehouse in Gary. It used to be an old steel mill. Them guns was supposed to go to my nigga Screwly G, but I'ma let you get em. Kevlar vests, Dracos, ARPs, Hellpups, Glocks with switches and all kinda extended clips and drums — enough firepower to level a project building. I'll have my people drop the location to your phone in an hour."

Hard nodded, a grim sense of purpose settling into his bones. "I appreciate you, bruh. More than you know. On Vice Lord."

"Just be careful, Big Homie," Markio warned. "Don't let these lil niggas send you back to that cage. Do what needs to be done, clean up the mess, and get back to that woman who been holding you down these past couple years."

"I ain't going back," Hard promised. "That's on my soul."

He ended the call and immediately dialed Tone Bone.

The FaceTime picked up, but Tone wasn't in a jet. He was in a basement, the lighting dim and yellow. The camera was propped up on a workbench. Tone's fat dreadlocks swung over his shoulders as he worked with mechanical precision, sliding rifle shells into a 100-round drum magazine for his AR pistol. The clack-clack-clack of the springs was the only music he needed this morning. He was a very serious man in times of war. In the nineties he'd participated in a number of Chicago gang wars right alongside Hard, and not once had he folded under pressure.

"You heard anything new?" Hard asked.

Tone Bone didn't look up from the drum, but his jaw was set tight. "I been on my phone all morning. I reached out to my lil bitch in Southgate, the one whose sister was bringing you all them phones. She said Thirty and Trey didn't go home last night. They're ducked off right now, but Michigan City is a small pond, Hard. They can't stay underwater forever."

Hard stood up, catching his reflection in the bathroom mirror. The man looking back at him wasn't the reformed gangster who wanted peace. It was the man who had earned the name Hard.

"Today is the day, Tone," Hard said, his voice a grim reaper's whisper. "I don't care about that parole. I don't care about the law. I want both of 'em. I want the driver and the shooter."

"I'm already loaded up, bruh," Tone Bone replied, finally looking into the camera with eyes that held no mercy. "Just tell me where to meet you at. By tonight, Thirty and Trey gon' be talking to the devil."

Chapter 11

The morning air in Michigan City was a biting gray shroud as HJ stood in the mouth of a narrow East Side alley. His breath came in ragged plumes of steam, his eyes fixed on the matte black Suburban. It looked like a discarded shell, its tires buried in the dirty slush, its body riddled with the jagged entry wounds of Lorde's Draco.

"Engine was hit several times. I'm surprised it made it this far," a voice called out behind him.

HJ turned to see Detective Richard Miller, a man who'd spent thirty years navigating the grime of the city. Miller was holding a tablet, his face set in a grimace of professional annoyance.

"Just got the hit, Gaing. Thirty reported this thing stolen twenty minutes before the first shot was fired at your pops' house. Typical play. He's already building his alibi in paper. Probably some shit he saw on an episode of Law and Order."

HJ slammed his hand against the cold metal of the SUV. "We both know he was behind the wheel, Miller. My little brother's bullets are all in the inside of this door, and there's blood all over the backseat. Have you checked the hospital?"

"St. Anthony's emailed us. A guy named Derrick Tyson, who goes by Big Block, was dumped at the ER entrance shortly after the shooting at your family's place. Two bullet wounds, bleeding like a stuck pig," Miller said, scrolling through the report. "But the man's a liar. He told the patrol officers he was walking to the corner store and got caught in crossfire from a 'passing car.' Claims he didn't see a thing. Won't even give us a name for who dropped him off."

HJ felt the walls closing in. The street code was holding firm, shielding the animals who had taken his niece's life. He gritted his teeth and kicked a frozen Cheetos bag across the alley.

"There's more," Miller added, leaning against the fender of Thirty's 'stolen' SUV. "Last night, right after the heat died down, a pink Escalade practically crashed into the precinct parking lot. Belonged to a surgeon, Tyrisha Tanner. The truck was shot to hell. One of the passengers was Trey. He told the responding officer—off the record, mind you—that he thinks his girlfriend, Vielle Gaing, was the one who chased and shot at them. He's also saying she's the one who shot him the other night. He's trying to flip the script, making her look like the aggressor to justify whatever he did earlier."

The mention of Vielle's name made HJ's blood run cold. She was out there, alone, playing a game she couldn't win against a man like Trey. Sure, she was a street girl through and through, having spent many of her formative years in the slums of Houston, Texas, but HJ had read Trey's file. Trey and his family were originally from the South Side of Chicago, and they were closely affiliated with the Black Disciples street gang. In fact, Trey had admitted to being an actual member of the gang during his last DUI arrest; HJ had seen the bodycam footage. The BDs were a particularly violent bunch, especially the younger ones.

And Vielle had shot one of their most respected members.

"Trey's the triggerman," HJ said, his voice dropping to a dangerous whisper. "Thirty provides the muscle and the car, but Trey is the one with the ego. He's the one who couldn't handle getting shot in that parking lot. I knew it had something to do with my sister. I fucking knew it."

"If you find him first, Gaing, you gotta bring him in," Miller warned, his eyes searching HJ's face for any sign of the "old man" Hardis. "Don't do something that costs you that badge. Journee wouldn't want her uncle in a cell right next to her killer. You with me?"

HJ didn't answer. He turned and walked back to his Ford Explorer, his mind already calculating the next move. He didn't care about the badge anymore; the badge hadn't protected his little sister's house on 7th Street. He knew the East Side like the back of his hand, and he wondered where Trey's "side chick" would take a man who needed to stay off the radar.

He pulled out his burner phone, the one he never used for police business, and sent a single text to a confidential informant on Michigan Boulevard.

'Looking for a bullet-riddled pink Escalade. Five bills for a confirmed location.'

He wasn't hunting as a detective anymore. He was hunting as a Gaing. He threw the Explorer into gear and peeled out of the alley, his hazel eyes scanning every driveway and tucked-away garage. Trey thought he was safe behind a surgeon's coat and a stolen car report, but he had no idea that a grieving uncle with a state-issued Glock was currently tearing the city apart to find him.

Chapter 12

From his bedroom window Hard could see that Vee's neighbors and other good-hearted locals had already begun placing teddy bears and supportive signs on the snow-caked sidewalk in front of the house. He'd stood and watched as a single black mother and her two young daughters laid flowers at the foot of the porch steps. A news van from the Northwest Indiana Times was parked across the street the last time he looked out there. He hoped to God they wouldn't be waiting to ask him questions when it came time for him to leave out.

Hard had been up for hours, the adrenaline of the previous night's carnage replaced by a cold, calculating stillness. He had scrubbed the blood of his granddaughter from his skin, but the stain on his soul was permanent. Now, his priority was the living.

He entered the bedroom carrying a heavy wooden tray, the aroma of maple syrup, fried catfish, and buttery grits trailing behind him. Candy was still buried under the duvet, a soft mound of feminine curves.

"Morning, baby," Hard said.

Candy didn't stir.

Hard set the tray down on the nightstand, and the clink of silverware against porcelain finally drew Candy from her sleep. She blinked, her hair a wild, lustrous halo against the soft white pillows, and her eyes found him. For a split second, the warmth in her eyes made the room feel like the sanctuary they'd intended it to be.

But then she saw his eyes — cold, tired, and devoid of the joyful glow he'd carried when he walked out of prison last night.

"You didn't sleep at all, did you?" she whispered, sitting up and pulling the sheet to her chest.

"I slept enough," Hard lied. He sat on the edge of the bed, handing her the plate. "Eat up. You got a long ride back to Indianapolis. As soon as I go and see my parole officer I want you to drive back to Nap and stay there until I get all this shit figured out."

Candy began to eat, but her eyes never left Hard's. She looked a lot like Rihanna in the face, only she had a body like Cardi B. She'd paid almost ten grand for her perfectly round fat ass. Her sleepy eyes regarded him skeptically.

"You just got out, bae. I mean, you just got out. I'm not about to let you go back. I can't just sit back and let you do that."

"Them niggas killed my granddaughter. I'm not letting that go. I can't." He ran a hand forward over his bald scalp. He had his HARD chain on. The diamond watch on his wrist read the time as being 7:18 AM. "I just met my grandbaby not even an hour before she died. Ain't no way I'm letting that slide. I'm sending Trey to the sky with her as soon as I see him."

Candy sighed. She ate her breakfast in relative silence after that, and when she went into the bathroom to shower she locked the door to keep Hard out. He heard the metallic click of the lock engaging from his seat on the bed, but he didn't get up to confirm his suspicion. Instead he used the alone time to contact a local contractor and get a rough estimate on how much it would cost to fix the damage to his daughter's home.

He'd already showered himself. Now he wore an all-white Sinew hoodie over matching sweatpants and fresh white Nike Air Force Ones. He thought the white made his jewelry stand out in amazing clarity , and despite his grief, he felt refreshed by the heavenly color. Blessed, so to speak.

He took twenty grand out of his backpack and stuffed it down in his right-hand pants pocket. Flower had texted him saying she was out of the hospital and on her way back to her place in Chicago with Leroy "Spark Boy" Oliver, the Four Corner Hustler who was the father of her youngest son. Hard could think of nothing to say — his brain overflowed with thoughts of bloody vengeance — so he simply replied with a couple of emojis, a black heart and the okay sign.

When Candy came out of the bathroom half an hour later she was fully dressed in a pair of skintight blue jeans and a red-and-white Indiana University college sweater. Hard tossed her a ten-thousand-dollar bundle of hundreds from his backpack. She caught it in the air and regarded him with a hard and accusatory stare. The only makeup she had on was a thin coating of brick-red lipstick, and that was all she needed. Her thick red IU skullcap covered the top halves of her ears. Her thighs looked so tantalizingly thick behind the denim that for a moment Hard forgot all about his troubles.

"You don't have to pay me to go away," she said. "You can't bribe me with money."

"It ain't no bribe. I want you to go shopping. I feel like I owe you that much."

"The only thing you owe me is your continued freedom. I did not drive back and forth from Indianapolis every two weeks just to see you go right back to prison when you got out. I thought you was the big dog. I thought you had all kinds of young niggas to handle this type of shit for you. Why are you putting yourself on the line for something you can easily have somebody else do for you?"

Hard looked at his diamond Rolex again. It was 7:40.

"We need to get outta here if we gon' make this parole appointment at eight-thirty," he said.

Candy rolled her pretty eyes and scooped up her purse. She took out her pistol, checked the slide, and then wedged it in the back of her jeans.

Two minutes later they walked out the front door. Hard paused to ogle his red Corvette before climbing into the passenger seat of Candy's Durango. He couldn't wait to get behind the wheel of that beast.

She handed him her gun as she settled in behind the wheel, and they listened to Kendrick Lamar and Sza while they waited for the engine to warm. Hard was alert the entire time, incessantly flicking his eyes from one end of the block to the other — anything to keep his gaze off the heart wrenching memorial his neighbors had built in front of the house.

"I'm getting you an Airbnb," Candy told him as she drove off down 7th Street. "It can be somewhere nearby, but I don't want you living here after what happened last night."

"Gotta ask my P.O. first, but I'm with it." Hard brought up the direction to the parole office on his iPhone 17 and set it on the center console for Candy to see. "I ain't really tryna live right there anyway. That's right around the corner from where that nigga they accused me of killing lived. His whole family from out here. I don't wanna run into no issues while I'm on this parole."

"It's the ghetto, too. We got enough money to put you up somewhere nice, somewhere you don't have to be worried about running into none of your enemies."

Hard nodded his agreement and sat back in his seat. He felt more than a little nervous with the Glock on his lap but he felt safe too. If there was one thing he'd learned how to do as a young gangster in Chicago, it was how to shoot a gun.

He checked the text messages on his iPhone 16 and saw that Bo had already messaged him.

'Have fun out there brotha. I hope you enjoyed yourself last night. Don't forget about the kid.'

Hard replied: 'I could never forget about my brothers. About to add myself to your GTL contacts so you can message me even if you lose that phone. I'll text Ms. Jones and let her know the play, and I'ma get with my nigga Tone Bone in a few minutes to get you a pack together. Tell the bros I said undying love.'

Candy glanced over at him. "Who you textin'?"

"Bo Lord."

Candy smiled. She knew Bo well. She'd seen him in the cell with Hard too many times to count, and he was always sticking his face in front of the camera to say hi. Once she'd even tried hooking Bo up with one of her coworkers. That situation had ended terribly — the woman claimed Bo had threatened her over some money he accused her of stealing, and she'd called up to the prison about it, which resulted in his cell being searched and him being caught with a cell phone, a quarter pound of weed, and two ounces of heroin — but Bo had never blamed Candy for that, and she hadn't gotten upset with him, either.

"I still have him on my GTL contacts from that time you had me send him those videos," she said.

"I'm about to get him a lawyer, get my nigga out from under that hundred and fifteen years they sentenced him to."

"He deserves another chance."

Hard was nodding his head and googling attorneys when his phone rang with a FaceTime call from the Neek Neek, the mother of his detective son. This call he declined. Candy was an incredibly jealous woman when she wanted to be, and he didn't feel like going through the motions with her this morning.

"Since them boys gave you all that money," Candy said, "I'm assuming you gave me that stack of hundreds to spend on myself."

Hard only nodded. His nod put a glorious smile on his woman's face. She reached over and gave his knee an affectionate little squeeze.

"Nah, don't be touchin' all on me now." He jokingly pushed her hand away. "You just had a whole attitude with me before we left out."

"Because I don't want you going back to prison. The fuck? You should be glad I care enough to get mad at you in the first place."

Hard chuckled, nibbled at his bottom lip, and spent a couple of minutes staring out his window at the many homes and businesses they were passing by on their way to see his parole officer. Michigan City had changed so much in the years since he'd left the streets — of course it had; he'd been gone twenty years.

Candy reached over again. This time she interlaced the fingers of her right hand with those of his left. He raised the back of her hand to his mouth and pressed a gentle kiss against the soft, fragrant flesh.

God, it felt so good to be home.

Chapter 13

"They shot up my fucking truck, Trey! Your girlfriend tried to fucking kill us! No. No, I'm done. I can't do this anymore."

Trey waved her off. Tyrisha had a tendency to become overly dramatic when situations got tough, but right now Trey wasn't trying to hear it.

He swallowed another Percocet tablet and continued pacing a tight circle in Reesh's spacious kitchen. The Styrofoam cup in his left hand was filled with ice cubes, Sprite soda, and Tris Pharma promethazine and codeine syrup. He took another sip every couple of steps. The ache in his shoulder was now so numbed from the Lean and Percocets that he couldn't feel it at all.

Word of the drama he'd gotten himself into these past few days had spread to his boys in Chicago. He and his family were originally from Parkway Gardens, a sprawling apartment complex located on the boundary of the Greater Grand Crossing and Woodlawn areas, just east of Englewood. Three carloads of Black Disciples had pulled into Reesh's driveway just over an hour ago, and now three of the eight young black men who'd occupied those two vehicles were seated around Tyrisha's expensive Macassar Ebony kitchen table with half a dozen handguns and Draco pistols spread out in front of them.

Their official nicknames were OTF Rello, OTF Dank, and OTF Maeski. The diamond OTF pendants that hung from their thin gold-and-diamond necklaces were gifted to them by King Von himself shortly before his death as a reward for the brazen broad-day murder of a rival "Jaro City" Gangster Disciple they'd chased down and killed on 62nd and Vernon Avenue. All three of them had arrived wearing black"Shiesty" masks on their heads, leaving only their eyes exposed to the elements. Now those masks were off, exposing their dreadlocks and the many gang-related tattoos scrawled across their faces and necks.

Reesh and Thirty stood near the fridge, a typical location for people of their shape and size. Thirty had his fat fist stuffed down in a tube of barbecue-flavored Pringles. Tyrisha was wiping grease from her freshly manicured fingers. She had already eaten four of the ten big breakfast burritos she'd cooked them for breakfast, and Trey figured she would likely end up eating the remaining two he'd set aside for himself.

"So the bitch just up and shot you for no reason?" Maeski asked. He had just fired up a blunt of exotic weed and was holding the smoke in his lungs, which gave his voice a harsh, strangled sound.

Trey ignored the question and said, "I wouldn't even be out here if it wasn't for Thirty. On David, bro asked me to move out here so he could have a spot outside of the city. Got me livin' in a small-ass one-bedroom apartment when he got a whole fuckin' mansion in Chicago Heights."

"It's being renovated," Thirty explained. "Should be able to move in by the end of January. And shit, you act like you the only nigga livin' in that dusty-ass apartment. I'm sleepin' on the couch, nigga! Fuck is you talkin' about."

Trey didn't reply, he just kept pacing the floor, so Thirty sailed on:

"Plus, we got them projects on lock now. Look at how much bread we bringin' in from Southgate alone. Every nigga, every bitch who smoke weed out there, who they come and buy it from? Huh? Who they come and buy it from? Us! That's who. They buy it from us! I sell a half pound every day in them projects. Not to mention the pills we get rid of out there. Moving you out there was a damn good move, and you can't tell me no different. We makin' three and fo' thousand dollars a day.Because of them projects, we got enough bread to move to Calabasas if we want to."

Trey stopped pacing and glowered at his older brother. "That's good, because that's where we need to be going. Cala-fuckin'-basas. 'Cause we goin' to jail if we stay out here."

"You wanna run?" Small bits of chips sprayed from Thirty's mouth as he spoke. "Do you know how guilty that's gon' make us look? We ain't done shit, right? And you on probation. That probation officer ain't lettin' you move outta state. You see how they did Hard. Vee said they refused to let that nigga move back to Chicago, and that's where he from! The fuck you think they gon' say to you?"

"Probation different than parole."

"No it ain't. It's the same goddamn shit. You stuck here just like he is."

Shaking his head, Trey went to the table and sat down. Tyrisha came over to stand beside him. She was wearing way too much perfume, but it smelled good, so Trey didn't mention it.

I know the police done figured out who shot up that house, he thought to himself. *And Vee's brother is a fuckin' police officer. A detective. Shit.*

"You still ain't told me why this bitch shot you," Maeski said, passing the blunt to Rello. "Why she tweak like that, folks? Yo' ass did some'n. On David, you did some'n to make her pop yo' ass."

Rello and Dank laughed. Maeski tried laughing and ended up coughing his lungs out.

Tyrisha said, "So it was y'all who killed that baby last night?"

Everyone turned to her, and for a long time nobody said a word. Her mouth was still greasy from the last burrito she'd gulped down. She was wearing a silky, multicolored kimono and a yellow Chanel bonnet. Everybody else wore black from head to toe.

Finally, Rello said, "Check your girl before she fuck around and get us all booked."

"Baby, go." Trey put down his cup and pointed. "Go back there and lay down. And don't tell nobody nothin'."

Tyrisha sucked a tooth, as most Black women are prone to do when they feel like they've tried, but she walked around the table and left the kitchen, moving swiftly in her plush white Chanel slides.

Trey leaned back in his chair, thinking about Thirty's big house in the Heights and wishing he was there instead of being stuck here in Michigan City, Indiana. Thirty's house was in the Country Club area of Chicago Heights, right off Country Club Road. It was a classic two-story colonial with five bedrooms, four full bathrooms, and a nice-sized three-car garage where Thirty's 2024 Mercedes Maybach GLS 600 was parked alongside his customized 1972 Buick Electra 225. Tadda Mae, the retired stripper who'd given birth to two of Thirty's five children, lived in the nearby village of Olympia Fields. Her older sister was a renowned interior designer, so Thirty had put them in charge of overseeing the renovations.

"I wanna go out there so bad," Trey said, thinking out loud. "That nice-ass crib." He shook his head again. Sipped some more of his purplish-red narcotic drink. When he spoke again it was in a low whisper. "Got me out here blowin' niggas cribs down and shit, killin' kids. If twelve book us for that shit we cooked. On bro. On Lil Steve grave."

"So we at war with the Travelers now?" Dank asked. He was almost as fat as Thirty and blacker than everyone else in the room. "I know Hard from Rockwell Gardens, but he rock with shorty n'em off 16th, them Dark Side niggas. They got military guns. You know they got some real-deal rich niggas behind 'em. Bulletface plugged in with them niggas, and Markio from over there, too."

"I wouldn't give a fuck who Hard got ridin' with him." Trey picked up his Micro Draco pistol. It was a heavy little weapon, all steel and wood, fifteen and a half inches long with a 40-round clip full of 7.62 millimeter rifle shells. "It's up there now. That old ass nigga gon' die when I catch up with him. Him, his daughters, his sons, them puss' ass Vice Lords. Think I care 'cause one of his sons the police? I don't give a fuck about that shit. That nigga can die, too."

"On fo'nem grave," Maeski and Rello said simultaneously.

Trey yelled for the others to join them, and the five young shooters who'd been lounging in the living room spilled into the kitchen seconds later. OTF Flip, OTF Scooda, Front Street Killa, Front Street Dune, and OTF Fat Pockets. Trey knew them all, had gone to school with three of them, and he knew that every single one of them had killed before. Thirty turned on some music — King Von's "War With Us" — and soon the room was filled with weed smoke, conversation, and laughter.

The Gaing family had some serious trouble on their hands.

Chapter 14

Hard rarely ever came across men who were taller than he was.

Keith Mensah was one of those rare exceptions.

He was brown like coffee with a teaspoon of creamer, with a huge bulbous nose and prescription eyeglasses that he kept pushing up on the bridge of that abnormally fat beak of his. His lips were equally thick, and they were incredibly moist, as if he'd emptied a full tube of Carmex onto them just two or three minutes ago. Hard estimated his height to be somewhere in the neighborhood of six-eight, and he weighed every bit of three hundred and fifty pounds. He was ill-built, clearly out of shape, but Hard got the impression that there was a lot of rock-hard muscle under that flabby exterior.

"Have a seat," the giant parole officer said in the deepest of voices. He extended a huge hand, palm up, and motioned toward one of the chairs in front of his desk. "I ain't gon' piss test you today. Hell, after what you went through last night, I wouldn't be surprised if you showed up high as a kite."

Hard gave the big man half a nod and sat down in the chair. Mensah sat down next, and he spent half a minute studying his newest parolee's attire.

"That real?" Mensah asked and pointed at Hard's chain. "Are those real diamonds?"

Hard looked down at the pendant that spelled out his name in glistening white ice. "I believe it is. Didn't buy it myself, but..." He shrugged one shoulder and looked back up at his parole officer. "Pretty sure it's real. One of my guys gifted it to me as a welcome home present."

"The watch, too?"

"The watch, too. I guess they got a li'l love for me, I don't know. I'm definitely appreciative. Before I got out the joint I had only seen this kinda ice in Hip Hop magazines. Kite, XXL, Go Viral, Straight Stuntin' — shit like that."

Mensah consulted his computer for something. His swivel chair appeared to be fairly new, but it squawked and cried every time he moved. Walking in, Hard had seen a number of other male P.O.'s, all of them white men dressed professionally in button-up shirts and slacks over shiny black or brown dress shoes, but Mensah didn't abide by the same dress code. He was casual in a dark black turtleneck sweater, fitted blue jeans, and a black-and-blue pair of Air Jordan 11s that had to be at least a size eighteen. He wore a necklace too, a thin gold rope with a gold cross pendant. And he was chewing a stick of Big Red gum.

"I see here thaaaaat..." Mensah trailed off, still eyeing his computer screen, maneuvering the mouse with his left hand and repeatedly tapping the forefinger of his right hand on his desk. "Yeah. Yeah. Yeah, I see here that you're a Vice Lord. A leader of the Vice Lords. Mmm hmm."

"Retired, brotha."

"I ain't cha brotha." He shot a glance at Hard. "You and me, we are the furthest thing from being brothas. You can save that for someone who gives a damn. I'm telling you now, it's not in your best interest to pull that black card BS with me. I am your parole officer, and I will not hesitate to send your black ass right back to Indiana State Prison."

Hard knitted his brow and said nothing. But he did think something. That thought was Bitch ass nigga! But of course he couldn't give voice to such a thought.

"Nice-lookin' woman you got out there," Keith Mensah went on, as if he hadn't just snapped at Hard five seconds ago. "She get her body done? One'a them BDL's, or whatever you call it? If she did it looks good on her. Damn good. Mmm hmm."

"I need to move out of that house you got me down as livin' in." Hard scratched at an itchy spot on the back of his bald head.

"You can do that. Yes sir, after what happened to your granddaughter last night, I'd be a cold dog to deny you that. Find yourself somewhere else to stay and get the address to me by the end of next week. Next Friday. Let me see that phone'a yours."

Hard's eyes doubled in size, but only for a second or two. Roughly half of the numbers saved to the contacts list in his iPhone 16 belonged to men who were incarcerated and in possession of illegally obtained cell phones. There were text messages on WhatsApp pertaining to criminal gang activity, trafficking contraband into prison, and several other incriminating topics. If he handed his phone over to his bipolar parole officer he would almost certainly be sent right back to prison.

But then he had an epiphany: the brand-new iPhone 17. There weren't any phone numbers saved in that phone, and he had it in the belly pocket of his hoodie.

He pulled it out and handed it over. Mensah went all through it, searching for something he most assuredly was not going to find.

"I can tell you been gone a long time," Mensah said. "Look like all you done used on here is Google Maps. Anybody else would've had seventy-nine different apps downloaded by now."

"I ain't got time for all that." Hard cracked a nervous smile. "Been with my family ever since I got home."

"Hear anything about who might've behind that shooting?"

Hard wagged his head from side to side. "Not a clue."

Mensah typed something into the phone and then handed it back. "I put my number in there. My cell phone number.

You text me that address as soon as you find yourself somewhere else to stay."

"Will do."

"And don't let me hear nothin' about you tryna go after the boys who did that to your granddaughter. You let the law deal with that whole business. I know HJ. He's a good man, a good detective, and you can bet your ass that he ain't gon' rest until he finds out who killed his niece. The whole police force'll be on top of that. You just sit back and let justice prevail."

Hard offered another half nod. His watch read the time as being 8:43 AM. He had twenty thousand dollars in his pocket and twenty thousand vengeful ideas in his brain.

"Go on and get." The Big man rose from his creaky swivel chair and extended his hand for a shake. Reluctantly, Hard shook it. "And remember what I said."

"How could I forget? Seriously. Either I fall back and stay out or get involved and go back to prison. Ignorant decisions get ignorant results."

"Every time," Mensah concurred.

"I'll see you soon, Hardis. Keeping you and your family in my prayers."

"Thanks, big man."

Hard turned and left the office. He went back the way he came and found Candy right where he'd left her, sitting in the little waiting area with a People magazine open on her lap and a Snickers bar open in her hand.

She looked up at him and smiled. "Jennifer Lawrence is pregnant!"

Hard gave her a look that could have been best described by using his nickname.

"Jennifer Lawrence," she repeated. "You know, from The Hunger Games. She's pregnant." Candy held up the magazine for emphasis, and when Hard didn't respond she rolled her eyes and got up from her chair. "Grumpy old man."

Hard hurried out of the office building and made a beeline for the Durango.

"Where's Lorde?" Candy asked from behind him. She had to speed-walk to keep up with him.

"Prob'ly somewhere out here lookin' for them niggas. You know he lost two people last night. He grew up with Baby Lord. That was one of Markio's boys, too. Them li'l niggas played with fire last night. We finna set this whole city ablaze over my grandbaby. You can bet your bottom dollar on that."

Chapter 15

Money Gang Entertainment was the official name for Baby Gang's clique. It began as a two-man rap group — Baby Gang and Anfernee "P Money " Peterson, friends since their middle school days at Krueger — and turned into a West Side street gang with over thirty official members. Many of them were in different organizations — for instance, Baby Gang was a Conservative Vice Lord while P Money was a Piru Blood — and their beefs usually stemmed from robberies and drug deals with guys from other cities and neighborhoods.

This was the first time Money Gang had started beefing with another gang over a bitch.

It began with a Snapchat video Meko had posted the previous night. The video started in Bambi's living room, giving his more than eighteen hundred followers a courtside view of Tonya and Kela bouncing their asses to Cardi B, and it ended with Meko standing outside Bambi's bedroom door, laughing and smiling at the sexual noises coming from the other side.

"Trey better come get his bitch," Meko said to the camera. "Baby Gang out here slayin' hoes."

That video had more than four thousand views in a matter of minutes, so it was no real surprise to Money Gang when Trey and his squad of Black Disciples got wind of it. It was also no surprise when Trey responded in his Instagram Story with a simple three-word text: Fuck Money Gang.

What did come as a surprise was the moment the two gangs rode past each other on Michigan Boulevard, just as they were passing the GoLo gas station at the Vail Street intersection.

Baby Gang was behind the wheel of his mother's blacked-out Kia Telluride, on his way to see her in a neighborhood Michigan City natives were fond of calling Deep Lakeland; Trey and his gang occupied a dark green Jeep Grand Cherokee Trackhawk, a black BMW X5, and a red Dodge Charger SRT, and they were simply "sliding," i.e. searching for Vielle's father and brothers so they could do to them what Trey had done to Vee's west side home.

Meko saw them first. He was in the passenger seat beside BG, eyes on the road, and he stared down the three vehicles as they barreled past in the southbound lane. It was the sight of Trey in the passenger seat of the Trackhawk that snagged Meko's attention.

"There go dat nigga Trey right there." Meko pointed with his Glock pistol, which had been modified with a sear switch that turned it into a machine gun.

At the same time, Trey and his boys stared back. Baby Gang laughed out loud, thinking That's why I fucked yo' bitch, you fuckin' goofy, and then his thoughts were cut short, because Trey rose up out of the sunroof and sprayed the Telluride with a fully-automatic Glock pistol.

BG ducked low and floored it. Glass blew out all around him. Bullets pinged and whizzed through the SUV like metal bumblebees.

Unafraid, Meko raised his Glock 17 and shot back. He had a 40-shot extended magazine, a "Vec," and he wasted no time peppering all three vehicles with gunfire, even as the men inside those vehicles returned fire.

One block up Baby Gang made a screeching right turn onto Cleveland Avenue.

"Spin this bitch!" Meko screamed, spittle flying from his enraged mouth. "Spin this bitch!"

BG made another right turn onto Tremont Street and a few seconds later he made a third right turn that put him on Poplar, right in front of the GoLo.

By then Trey and his boys had made a U-turn to chase after Money Gang. They were just speeding past the intersection, looking ahead instead of glancing to the side street on their right, which made it easy work for BG and his boys to jump out with their guns all trained on the sides of the three speeding vehicles.

Baby Gang, Shaggy, and Meko all started shooting their Glocks. Brrrrrr…Phop, Phop, Phop, Phop, Phop, Phop, Phop…Brrrrrr…Brrrrrrrrr…

An enfilade of gunfire swept across the passenger's side of the Jeep, the BMW, and the Charger, and the BMW veered leftward to slam nose-first into a lamppost that had an American flag sticking up out of it. That flag went cartwheeling across the street, the lamppost tipped over, and the BMW spun two full rotations before coming to a stop.

Shaggy lowered his gun and cupped his free hand against his stomach. He was hit. Dark red lifeblood spilled from between his splayed fingers.

"They shot me," he said. His eyes were wide with disbelief. Baby Gang saw another bullet wound in Shaggy's left forearm, right through the forehead of his Benjamin Franklin tattoo, but Shaggy only seemed to notice the stomach wound.

And the shootout wasn't over.

Baby Gang noticed that the Charger had come to a stop twenty or thirty feet away. So had the Jeep. Before he could fully process what that meant, the rear driver's side door of the BMW swung open and a masked gunman jumped out shooting a Draco.

Baby Gang raised his own Glock and let off half a dozen shots as he and his two road dogs backpedaled to the rear of the Telluride. Shaggy could no longer shoot, so he got behind the SUV and plopped down on his ass. More glass exploded.

Both tires on the passenger side hissed and went flat, causing the Telluride to lean toward that side.

And the gunshots kept coming.

How Meko managed to avoid being shot himself was a miracle only God could explain. He didn't let up at all; no ducking, no running. He did walk backwards to the rear of the Kia SUV with Shaggy and Baby Gang, but he was shooting his gun the entire time. He emptied his 50-shot drum, ejected it, and then he inserted a 30-round clip and started shooting again.

This morning was significantly warmer than the previous two days. There was snowmelt everywhere, creating great ponds of water that pooled on the sidewalks and flowed into the curbside sewer drains.

Other motorists sped off in every direction as the deafening rattle of semi-auto and fully automatic gunfire persisted. Baby Gang kept raising up to shoot, and every time he did it he saw those masked gunmen shooting back. One bullet came so close to his right ear that he heard the whistle and felt the burn.

The gunfire didn't die down until the welcoming shriek of police sirens sounded. Then and only then did Trey and his boys start preparing for an escape. Three masked gunmen who'd occupied the crashed BMW ran toward the Jeep and the Charger. One of them was limping, while another one was holding his bleeding right elbow.

Meko and Baby Gang watched them go with their guns lowered to their sides. Neither Meko nor Baby Gang were convicted felon, and since Indiana law made it legal for anyone over the age of eighteen to possess a firearm, they were in the clear. The only thing Meko had to do was disassemble his Glock switch before the police showed up.

"We gon' have to kill them niggas," Baby Gang said. He was frantic, breathing fast, his wide eyes darting left and right.

"On my baby," Meko said. He began removing his Glock switch, looking around at the few cars that hadn't sped off. "It's either gon' be us or them."

Chapter 16

Vielle awoke to an empty bedroom and a phone full of missed calls and new text messages. The curtains were open; sunlight poured into the room, bright and blinding. Dust motes swirled about in those beaming rays of sunshine. She tasted sex in her mouth, vestigial traces of semen and vaginal juices, and she felt drowsy from the weed and liquor she'd consumed.

She picked up her phone from the bedside table and stuck out her lower lip when she saw that she only had nineteen percent left on her battery.

Hard had called her twice, and like the old man he was he'd left a voicemail:

"Morning, baby girl. I just went and seen my P.O. The nigga seemed cool but he snapped at me a lil bit too. Bipolar, like you." He laughed once. "But nah, he gave me permission to move somewhere else 'cause of what happened last night. Me and Candy out looking for another place now. Find out how much it's gon' cost us to get all the repairs done and I'll pay for that shit myself. Give me a call when you get up."

Vee rolled her eyes. She wanted her daddy to stay with her. Leaving was understandable — who wanted to live in a house where their own grandchild had died? — but Vee wasn't about to let anybody run her out of her own house. Fuck that. She was staying. Insurance would cover the damages, and all that would be done today. She was going to invest in another gun — an AR-15 with all the accessories

— and the next time Trey or any of his boys came through she would be ready.

There were eight new text messages: one from Baby Gang, two from Flower, one from Lorde, two from Thirty's ex-girlfriend Tadda Mae, and one from HJ.

Baby Gang's message was exactly what Vielle wanted to hear: 'Shorty I'm really tryna fwu. On some relationship type shit. Just left to take my sister her car back, but I'll be back thru there later. Fwm.'

Flower's first text said she was already out of the hospital and back in Chicago, and the next text asked if Vee was okay and told her to call when she got up.

Lorde had sent a sad face emoji that brought tears to Vee's eyes as soon as she saw it, Tadda Mae wanted to know what was going on between Vee and Trey, and HJ wanted Vee to call him as soon as possible.

Vee sat up in bed and yawned. A hint of a smirk creased the corner of her mouth when she saw the clothes she'd taken off before showering all folded and cleaned at the foot of the bed. She smelled breakfast in the air, eggs and syrup and bacon, and that was all the motivation she needed to get out of bed, step into her shoes, and head out to the kitchen.

She passed Bambi and Kela in the living room. Bambi's boyfriend, Tink, was sitting right next to her on the sofa with a PlayStation controller in his hands and a half-eaten plate on the coffee table in front of him. He was playing his favorite game, Hitman 3, while Bambi sat beside him with her plate on her lap and a blunt in her hand. Kela was on the love seat, watching Tink play the game.

Tink who was at least fifteen years older than his teenage girlfriend.

"Your plate's in the microwave," Bambi said to Vee. "It should still be hot. I just put it in there."

"Where Tonya go?"

"To drop Jayla off at work and take Tiana home. They had came over in a Uber last night."

"I thought Tiana had a car," Vee muttered as she continued on into the kitchen.

"She do," Kela said. "That nigga Doug crashed her shit the other day. It's in the shop."

"That's exactly why I don't be lettin' niggas drive my shit. You ain't about to have my insurance all fucked up."

No one commented on that, so Vielle sat down to eat. She scrolled through Facebook while she chewed. Her inbox was filled with people asking questions about last night's shootings — the deadly one at her place and the one that had taken place on Michigan Boulevard shortly thereafter. A bunch of prayers and condolences. Her boss at Walmart had messaged her saying she understood if she didn't want to come to work today.

"You better fuckin' understand," Vee mouthed silently.

She left Messenger for her Facebook news feed and spent a few minutes scrolling through other people's lives while she chowed down on crispy strips of bacon, cheesy scrambled eggs, and buttery blueberry pancakes.

It was 10:17 AM, and she'd been scrolling for about ten minutes, when she made it to a video one of her Walmart coworkers had shared from someone else's page.

The video was chaotic. Whoever recorded had had screamed out in fearful panic the second they started filming, and she had good reason to scream. She was inside the GoLo gas station on Michigan Boulevard and Poplar, holding her phone up over a rack of potato chips and recording the broad-day shootout that was taking place outside. There was a black SUV parked in the middle of the street, and it was being hammered with gunfire. Vee immediately recognized the boy who was backing up on the driver's side of the SUV. It was Baby Gang, and he was shooting at something or someone off camera. Shaggy was behind him, walking backwards while clutching his stomach. There were so many rounds hitting the SUV that it was rocking on its frame.

"Shit, y'all! Come look at this!" Vee said in a wide-eyed shout. "Baby Gang just got in a shootout, and it look like Shaggy got shot!"

Kela was the first one at Vielle's side. Bambi was next, and Tink paused his game to look back at the girls.

Together the three young baddies watched the video from the beginning. Kela gasped when she saw Shaggy drop to the ground behind the bullet-riddled truck. The camera briefly panned over to the left, and they were able to see the crashed BMW truck and the masked gunman who leapt out of it wielding a Draco. Somebody shot him and he momentarily dropped to one knee, but he was back up in an instant, dumping round after round at Meko and Baby Gang.

They watched the video three times, back to back, and then Vielle left Facebook to phone Baby Gang. He didn't answer, so Kela tried calling Meko.

"They ain't answering," she said. "I wonder who they was shootin' at. I ain't never seen that BMW before."

"Me neither." Vee went to the sink and slipped her empty plate into a bath of dirty dish water. When she turned back to her girls they were staring at her expectantly.

"You think it was Trey n'em, don't you?" Bambi asked.

Vee shrugged. "I'm about to take a shower. Call up to the hospital and see if y'all can find out which room they got Shaggy in."

They did find out. Kela had gone to school with eighteen-year-old Talil "Shaggy" Wiggins, and her aunt was a nurse at St. Anthony's. Shaggy was currently in surgery. He'd been shot three times — in the lower abdomen, through the forearm, and in the hip.

One man had been found dead inside the BMW with a bullet wound to the head, and though the police were fairly certain that there were other shooting victims, no one else had shown up at the hospital.

Kela and Bambi told Vee all this through the bathroom door as she was showering and getting dressed in the same outfit she'd worn last night, a red-and-white Chanel bodysuit with matching leather high-heeled boots. It complimented her red hair and the gloss on her lips.

When she rejoined them in the living room she fingered the venetian blinds down and looked outside. There was an MCPD patrol car parked across the street. She could see a young-looking white man sitting behind the wheel. He glanced her way and she let go of the blinds to back up a couple of steps.

"Shit," she said. "Twelve."

Bambi's eyebrows went up, and she flattened one hand against her chest. Her eyes moved from person to person.

"Baby, go grab my dope," Tink said, rising to his feet.

Tink was brown like Bambi and skinny like Wiz Khalifa. Tall, too, and he was an original westsider, one of the few remaining members of the Dub Life Goons. Once upon a time he'd been friends with Blake "Bulletface" King, the former dope boy turned billionaire rap star. He still had the 2012 Mercedes Benz S550 Blake had gifted him way back then. He'd been robbed of his jewelry by a now-deceased Chicago rapper named Bloodhound Jeff, which was why Blake had cut him off, but he had that sexy ass Benz, and that got him all the girls. It was the only reason Bambi called him her man.

He'd bought a quarter kilo of cocaine from his Chicago connect a few days ago. He still had about seven ounces left, stashed in a Nike shoe box with a few thousand dollars in cash. Vielle knew all his business because Bambi told her everything.

"They might be here for me," Vee said. She was putting on her $8,500 red leather Chanel bomber jacket. It had a fur-lined hood that she pulled forward over her head. "I'm going out the back door. Bambi, get in my car and drive down to the end of the block on 8th. I'll meet you down there."

"Why would they be lookin' for you?" Tink asked.

"She shot up Tyrisha's Escalade last night. Trey was in the truck with her," Bambi said. "Sis damn near chased them into the police station parking lot."

Sometimes Bambi snitched without even meaning to.

"Are you listening to me?" Vee took her gun out of her purse and exchanged the mostly depleted 13-round magazine with a fresh 16-round ProMag clip she kept at the bottom of her purse. She cocked the slide back, chambering a round, and then tossed her keys to Bambi. "Start up my car, drive it to the end of the block, and wait for me there."

"Girl, I'm not even dressed, and they are not looking for you. How would they even know you're here? You don't live here."

"HJ knows where I hang out. That means the Michigan City Police Department knows where I hang out. If they're looking for me, you better believe he told them where to find me."

Bambi hesitated. Her small black shirt had Do you smell what the Rock is cooking? printed across the bottom below a picture of Dwayne "The Rock" Johnson standing in the ring on the corner turnbuckle in his wrestling underwear. Her barely there boy shorts had The Rock's bronco emblem printed across the ass.

She definitely wasn't dressed for December weather.

"Bitch, throw me my keys back," Vielle snapped, and the moment she caught them she was on her way.

She went through the kitchen and out the back door. There was a three-inch layer of snow from the back porch steps all the way down the walkway to the backyard fence, but it was melting quickly. Someone's dog was barking; Vee couldn't tell which direction the barks were coming from. She looked both ways as she trudged through the snow. At the gate she paused to answer her phone and was surprised to see that it was Trey calling.

Decline.

"Got me fucked up," she muttered and walked through the gateway.

She turned right and started toward 8th Street, keeping her head down and her hand in her purse, her fingers clenched tight around the butt of her pistol. Her phone rang with another FaceTime call from Trey, and this time she answered.

His cold scowl burgeoned into a devil's smile the instant he laid eyes on her. He was holding a Draco back against his shoulder, and Vee could tell from the background that he was in the backseat of a fast-moving vehicle. She could see cars and SUVs and one semi truck on the road behind him.

He was on the highway.

Probably Interstate 94.

On his way to Chicago, his hometown.

"Who you got holding that phone?" Vee asked. "I know it ain't you."

"It ain't that nigga you fucked last night, either." Trey chuckled dryly. The Draco went down and a blunt came up. He puffed and smirked. "What was his name again? Baby Gang? Whatever his name is, he might wanna check on his mans. I heard some niggas caught him in his sister truck and blew dat muhfucka down!"

His head fell back and he laughed like a maniac.

"You almost got caught, too. Don't act like your fat little girlfriend didn't get her pretty lil Escalade shot up last night. Scary ass bitch gon' drive to the police station. I know you told her to do that shit. Fuckin' coward."

The cherry at the end of Trey's blunt brightened as he puffed. He smirked again, but the expression seemed superficial. A simile of a smile.

"Shorty don't even know what he done did. They just killed a real member. We gotta go to the city to grieve wit' lil folks mama n'em, but on King David, bitch, as soon as we get back out here, niggas gon' die! Fuck is you talkin' 'bout?

A nigga gon' die every day until ain't nobody left. We already took two last night. I know one was a baby, but oh well. Shouldn't have been there. Wrong place at the wrong time. And I hear that nigga Shaggy in critical. He might be the third one."

He held up three fingers, brought them to his mouth, kissed them, and then blew smoke toward the roof above him.

His blatant disregard for her niece's life brought tears of pure hatred to Vielle's eyes. She clenched her teeth and flared her nostrils. Her forefinger tightened against the trigger of her gun, and she had to take her hand off the handle to keep from shooting a hole through her purse.

"I don't know how I ever loved you, Trey. I really don't ." Vielle sniffled and wiped away the hot tears that were trickling down her face. This morning was warmer than yesterday had been, but her breaths still came out in smoky puffs. "You got the right family, though. I can tell you that now. Karma's a bitch. You'll get what you got comin', and I mean reeeeeal soon. You just wait and see. You just wait and fuckin' see."

The blurp of a police siren made Vee raise her head, and she wasn't a bit surprised to see that HJ's dark blue Explorer had turned into the alley and was driving straight toward her. The patrol car she'd seen parked across the street from Bambi's house was now rolling up behind her.

She looked down at her phone to end the call and saw that Trey had already hung up. Her hands were shaking with rage as she dropped the phone into her purse.

We gon' catch yo' mothafuckin' ass, Trey, she thought to herself. *One way or the other, we're gonna catch you. And when we do…*

"Sis, sis, sis," HJ said, shaking his head as he stepped out of his truck. "What do you have going on out here? Please tell me what I'm hearing is a lie."

Vielle didn't say a word. She had the right to remain silent, and right now seemed like the best time to make use of that right.

"Gotta take you in, sis." He went behind her and snapped a pair of cuffs onto her narrow wrists. "I got two people saying they saw you shooting at them last night, and we got your car on a traffic cam chasing after them."

Again Vee said nothing. She allowed HJ to walk her to the back door of his Explorer, and he patted her down and confiscated her purse she climbed in without a hassle.

"I'm hurt too, sis." HJ stood there in the open doorway, leaning in. "That was our niece who died on that floor last night. I'm just as upset as you are. But you should've let me do my job. Going after them on your own was the wrong move, Vee. Now you're the one being arrested."

"You know who killed her, and yet you're out here tryna lock me up." She sniffled. More tears fell. HJ put a consoling hand on her shoulder and she shook it off. "Don't fuckin' touch me."

HJ stared at her for a moment. Then he sighed and shut the door.

Vielle cried silently in the backseat of her oldest brother's unmarked SUV,and she didn't say a single word all the way to the police station.

Chapter 17

"Yes. Oh my God, yes! This is it. This is where I want to live."

Hard massaged his tired eyes and sat forward in the passenger seat to look out at the house his girlfriend was so amped up about.

After visiting his parole officer in downtown La Porte, Hard and Candy went house hunting in the same town. Candy had immediately phoned Lakita Thomas, a local real estate agent who'd gained notoriety not only because of her exceptional paintings but also because she had once dated Grammy -winning rap artist Bulletface. Now she was listed among the top five percent of successful real estate agents in Northwest Indiana. Lakita was away on business, but she'd sent her protégé, her younger cousin Tamia, to assist them in finding a home.

The house they were looking at was located in La Porte's Concord Vineyard subdivision. It sat on a cul-de-sac at the end of a long, paved driveway on Riesling Court. The house was a two-story gray stone with a high-pitched roofline and multiple gables, giving it a stately, imposing silhouette that felt like a fortress compared to the house on the west side of Michigan City. The two-car garage was constructed of earth-toned brick. The front yard consisted of a meticulously mulched flower bed, three young maple trees, and a collection of decorative boulders.

It was the kind of house that practically screamed "American Dream."

Tamia pulled her matte black Lincoln Navigator into the driveway and Candy eased in to park beside her.

"My house in Avon is nice," Candy said, "but this…Oh my God! I would never leave."

Hard was bone-tired, but somehow he managed to get his face to smile. His phone was ringing on his lap. It took Candy pointing at it to get him to look down at it.

He answered the call as he was getting out of the truck. It was Tone Bone.

"Yeah," Hard answered.

"That nigga Trey just got in a shootout with Money Gang on Michigan Street."

"You mean Michigan Boulevard?"

"Yeah, yeah, that's it. Right by that GoLo. I'm out here in Southgate with this young bitch I met last time I came to visit you, and she told me everything. She said Thirty and Trey ain't been back to Trey's apartment since Vee's crib got shot up last night. She know that for sure 'cause she been waitin' on Thirty to get back so she could buy some loud. Somebody on her Facebook page shared video of the shootout, and they say some nigga named Baby Gang said it was Trey n'em he was shootin' at. They shot one of his Money Gang niggas and Money Gang killed one of theirs. Say they let off like two, three hun'ed rounds."

"Hold on one minute, Bone. I'm looking at this house."

"You moving out of the one they shot up, huh? Can't say I blame you."

"One minute, bruh."

Hard furrowed his brow. He walked around the truck and trailed the girls into the house at a distance, holding the phone to his ear, half listening to Tamia — a stunning little redbone in a sleek green pantsuit and high-end almond toe booties that gripped the snow good enough to keep her from slipping — as she introduced them to the property.

"Welcome to your potential new reality," Tamia said, her voice a melodic purr. She looked back and gave Hard a lingering, appreciative look that didn't go unnoticed by Candy, before turning to lead them toward the front door. The way her tailored pants hugged her curves made it clear she knew exactly how she looked from behind.

Inside, the $350,000 home opened into a bright, airy main floor that smelled of spiced vanilla.

"This is the heart of the home," Tamia said, gesturing with a manicured hand toward the great room. "You have these soaring vaulted ceilings and the gas fireplace, which — let's be honest — you'll likely be spending your snowy nights cuddled in front of."

She led them toward the gourmet kitchen, her hips swaying rhythmically as she navigated the hardwood floors. Candy looked back at Hard and rolled her eyes. He almost laughed.

"Look at these granite counters and the Shaker cabinetry. It's the perfect setup for some serious entertaining. Family, friends, coworkers — they'll all enjoy themselves in this beautiful room," she said, leaning slightly over the center island. She caught Hard's eye again. "Or maybe just a quiet, intimate breakfast for two."

At this Candy smiled. She did a slow spin, admiring the luxurious cabinetry, the stainless steel appliances, the smooth granite surfaces.

"I'll hit you back in a minute," Hard whispered into the phone. "Let me know if you hear anything about Trey and where that nigga might be hiding out."

"Yup. Mighty."

Tone Bone hung up, and Hard's attention went right back to the gorgeous little real estate agent. He had no urge to cheat on Candy — he was a one-woman kind of man, always had been — but there was no denying the woman's exceptional beauty.

She glided toward the French doors. "Through here is the tiered deck. It's covered in snow now, but come June, this is the perfect place in Concord Vineyard for a relaxing glass of wine, maybe a good book. I'm into those cheesy romance novels. If this place were mine, I'd be right here for at least an hour or two every night in the summer. Nice and quiet."

Hard nodded his head and did a little looking around himself. He'd been in some nice homes in the past, but that had been twenty years ago, when technology was practically in the Stone Age. Back then there were no smart stoves, smart refrigerators, smart lighting. This house was straight out of the future.

Tamia led them up the half-flight of stairs to the primary suite, her hips swaying, her presence filling the hallway. "This is my favorite feature," she said, stepping into a room that felt more like a high-end hotel. She pointed to a unique two-sided fireplace. "It connects the bedroom to the ensuite. You can see the flames when you're under the covers, and then again when you're soaking in the tub on the other side. This is what you call high-class living. It's all about the atmosphere."

Finally, she marched them down to the finished walk-out basement. "Some people just look at this as a basement, but it's really a second living space," Tamia explained, walking across the plush carpet toward the sliding glass doors that led to the backyard. "There's a full bathroom down here, another bedroom, and plenty of room for a home theater or... whatever other hobbies you two might have."

She turned back to them, leaning against the wet bar, a playful smirk dancing on her lips. "So, Hard, Candy…can you see yourselves living here, or do I need to show you something a little more 'adventurous'?"

The air in the basement was still, save for the low hum of the furnace and faint sound of Tamia's boots as she shifted her weight. Hard's phone rang again, this time with a call from HJ. He silenced it and spent a full minute looking around the basement, imagining what his man-cave might look like down here in the basement, and thinking about how nosy the neighbors in this semi-affluent subdivision might be. After twenty years in a tiny little prison cell, the half-million-dollar expanse of 4552 Riesling Court felt like a kingdom — one he intended to keep.

He looked at Candy, then back at Tamia. “It’s a nice place. Large. Quiet. Ducked off on a cul-de-sac, one way in and one way out.” He nodded, sucking on his bottom lip. “Yeah, I like it. We’ll take it.”

Tamia’s eyes shot up. “Just like that? No second walk-through?”

“I ain’t got time for a second nothin’,” Hard said, his voice firm and certain. “We have to move. Today, if that’s at all possible.”

Tamia leaned back against the wet bar, her eyes scanning him with a new level of interest.

“Moving that fast usually requires a cash offer to make the seller jump,” she said, her voice dropping an octave. “And we’d need to talk about the paperwork. Financing takes weeks, and I’m guessing yu aren’t looking to wait on a bank.”

He reached into the inner pocket of his Moncler jacket and brought out the twenty grand in hundred-dollar bills. He set it on the granite surface of the wet bar with a heavy thud. I got twenty racks right here. Another seventy in my backpack out there in the truck, and the rest will be coming from my account. But theirs is condition.”

Hard tilted his head toward Candy. “The house goes in her name. Tazera Williams. All of it. The deed, the title, the utilities. Everything.”

Candy blinked, her breath catching. “Hard, are you sure you want to do that? That’s a lot of trust to put in somebody.”

“You’re a nurse, baby. You the one with the clean record, the ‘good citizen’ credit score,” Hard said, taking Candy’s hand in his. “Me? I’m just a man tryna keep his head down. If the P.O. asks, you bought it with your savings and a “gift” you got from your family. Worst come to worst I’ll have

Markio vouch for the bread. I'm just the guy living here, helping with the lawn."

"Never seen a lawn man rocking a diamond Rolex on his wrist," Tamia commented with a seductive smile. She looked at the money, then at Candy. She knew the game. In real estate, money was green regardless of where it spent the last twenty years.

"A registered nurse with a stellar credit history moving into Concord Vineyard..." Tamia mused, a slow, knowing smile spreading across her face. "It's a perfect story, you ask me. I can write up the offer as a cash-heavy deal under Ms. Williams's name. It'll bypass a lot of the traditional red tape and get you the keys in record time."

Tamia walked over to Hard, stopping just inches from him. The scent of her perfume filled the space between them. She reached out, her fingers grazing the sleeve of his jacket as she picked up the stack of cash to tuck it into her bag.

"I'll need her ID and a few signatures to get the ball rolling," Tamia murmured, looking up at him through her lashes. "I can have the initial contract ready at my office in an hour. We'll keep it all very...'discreet'."

She turned to Candy, offering a professional smile. "Congratulations, Tazera. You're about to be a homeowner on Riesling Court. Safest neighborhood in the city. Heck, the county. The mayor lives a block over from here."

Hard nodded, the tension in his shoulders finally easing — at least for the moment. "Let's get it done. I wanna be moved in by sundown tomorrow."

Chapter 18

There was a gnat flying around the interrogation room, and it kept swooping down in front of Vielle's face. Every time she took a swing at it the fucker came back more aggressively.

"Fuck! Stupid ass gnat!"

She swatted at it again and missed again and the motherfucker came back again.

"Uuuggghh!"

They'd given her a bottle of water and her cell phone, but not her purse. They'd strip-searched her and fingerprinted her and confiscated her pistol for evidence. She had the feeling that the only reason she had her phone was because her brother was the city's leading homicide detective; either that or there was a microphone in the ceiling-mounted camera, and they wanted her to call someone and confess to the shooting the way all those rookie criminals did on The First 48.

That being said, she did the wise thing and phoned Karissa Mara, the lawyer she'd hired for a DUI charge she caught a few months back. She got the secretary and left a message. The secretary assured her that Mara would be contacting the jail within the hour to see if she had a bond. Vee hung up feeling down and alone, wishing she had a boyfriend she could call on at a time like this.

She was playing a game of solitaire on her phone when the faux wood door swung open ten minutes later. She looked up, saw a white female policewoman she'd never seen before, and went back to playing her game.

"Good morning, Vee. I'm Officer Steiner of the Michigan City Police Department. Got some questions about what happened on the Boulevard last night. You mind putting that phone down and giving me your attention for a couple of minutes? I'd hate to have to take it back."

Vielle sucked her teeth and looked up at the blue-eyed blonde. She was an attractive white woman, tall, slender, and comely. Her hair was drawn up in a flawless bun. A Pisces tattoo done in burgundy ink graced the space between the thumb and forefinger on her left hand. She smelled good, some kind of citrus-scented fragrance. She had a cute, innocent visage, reminding Vee of Sabrina Carpenter's gorgeous face.

"Don't call me that," Vielle said. "My name is Vielle. Call me that."

"That's fine by me. Vielle. What happened last night."

"The sun went down and another day started."

The cop flashed an amused smirk. "Good one." She nodded. Her bun bobbed back and forth. "Never heard that one before, and I've done a lot of interrogating."

Vee began cracking her knuckles. Officer Steiner hit the record button on her own smartphone and placed it on the table between them.

"Two nights ago a man named Treykwan Murray was shot in a parking lot inside the Southgate Apartments complex. He was taken to the hospital, and initially he refused to speak with the detectives who visited him in his hospital room. But last night, after he was shot at just up the street from here and chased almost into our parking lot, he gave a statement. He told Detective Corley it was you who shot him, and that it was also you who tried to kill him again last night."

"Did he tell you what he did? That he choked me and slapped me and…" She trailed off, realizing a second too late that she had perhaps said too much.

"No, he didn't. His version of events paint you as the aggressor. You got mad at him for liking some girl's pics. You punched him in the face and kicked him in the balls, and when he went out to try to get you to come back in out of the snowstorm, you shot him."

"Well, he's lying! The fuck?! That nigga got mad at me for liking and commenting under Baby Gang's pictures, and he slapped me. Choked me, too. He changed the story. I swear to God, he's changing the story. Making me look like the bad guy."

"That's why I need your side of the story, Vee…Elle. Vielle. Help me figure out what's going on here, because we're still trying to connect the dots in your niece's murder. And now we've had another shooting, this one on Michigan Boulevard. And can you guess who was involved in that? Victor Lewis, AKA Baby Gang. He and his boys got in a shootout with a group of men who jumped out of three different vehicles, all of them with Chicago license plates. One of the Chicago boys was killed, and judging from his tattoos he was in the same gang as Treykwan Murray. Coincidence?"

Vielle didn't know what to say to that, so she shook her head and rubbed one hand down her face.

"If Trey was behind your niece's murder, you need to be trying to help us get him off the streets. We have reason to believe that he may have been the triggerman, and if that's has case we have him on deadwood on two Level One murder charges and numerous counts of attempted murder. We may even be able to get your charges dismissed."

"What am I facing?"

"Right now? Three counts of attempted murder, criminal recklessness, reckless discharge of a firearm…"

"I didn't, ummm…I don't know." Vee was getting scared. "I think I need my lawyer. Yeah…yeah, I need to talk to my lawyer. I just called her. She's supposed to be coming up here to see me."

Steiner's friendly disposition became unfriendly. Her features hardened. She shut off the recorder, leaned forward on her elbows, and lowered her head, like a lioness stalking her prey in tall grass.

"HJ can't save your ass on this one, sweetheart. I'd advise you to get cooperative, and I mean fast."

"That wasn't me shooting at them last night, and when I shot Trey two nights ago it was in self-defense. Look at my neck. I still have the bruises."

Officer Steiner's pretty blue eyes dropped to investigate the bruising on Vielle's throat. Then she sat back in her chair and folded her arms across her chest. The pink flesh of her cheeks had darkened to a blush of red.

Several dark and ominous possibilities took hold of Vee's imagination. She saw herself in a cell block, wearing a striped jail uniform, eating slop off a thick brown plastic tray. She saw herself chained and shackled in court, looking up at an old white judge as her 100-year sentence was handed down. She saw herself growing old and gray, her family dying off while she rotted away in the Big House.

It was all too much to bear.

"Okay," Vee said, after a time. "What do I need to do?"

"You have your phone," Officer Steiner said, pointing at the iPhone for emphasis. "Give your ex a call. See if you can get him to incriminate himself."

Vielle looked down at her phone. She chewed at the inside of her bottom lip, tapping the toe of her shoe on the carpeted floor.

"Go ahead," Steiner encouraged. "Call him."

"Shit." Vee sighed.

Then she picked up her phone and dialed Trey's number.

Chapter 19

The sun was a hovering yellow globe above the Greystones across King Drive, shrinking the mounds of snow that lined the curb and spreading cold water across the asphalt.

Inside Parkway Gardens, the inner courtyard was a mix of cracked sidewalks and tough patches of grass that grew from the snow like mold. In the center, a rusted-out basketball hoop stood like a giant skeletal guard.

Seven of them were standing on the concrete steps of the 6412 entrance. The leader, a man called Devo, stood on the top step. His dreads were bleached at the tips, tied back in a messy bun that pulled at his scalp. He was one of the higher ranking Black Disciples from O Block, the Minister, and it was he who'd groomed Trey to be the gangster he'd grown to be. Devo was focused on his phone, the screen reflecting in his designer shades while he absently picked at the hem of his Dior hoodie.

Below him, Maeski and Dank were in the middle of an argument. Their hair — thick, waist-length ropes — swung like pendulums as they gestured. Maeski was leaning against a dented mountain bike, his locs partially covered by a crumpled Adidas beanie.

"Man, if you would'a bailed out right when Rello crashed the whip, bro wouldn't be fuckin' dead right now, gang," Maeski snapped. "Yo' bitch ass the reason folks dead, gang. On David."

Trey didn't chime in. He was on point, standing by the brick pillar where he had a clear line of sight through the breezeway toward the street. He kept flicking his dreads out of his face, his eyes scanning every car that slowed down on King Drive. "Stay on y'all square," he said to the gang. "Twelve just rode past. They might circle back."

His phone rang right then. He almost smiled when he saw it was Vielle calling.

Almost.

Front Street Dune and OTF Flip were both hospitalized at the University of Chicago Medical Center, and OTF Rello was dead. They had driven all the way back to Chicago before taking Flip and Dune to the hospital to keep from being charged in the Michigan City shooting. They'd driven the bullet-riddled Charger and Trackhawk to a McDonald's restaurant at the opposite end of Michigan Boulevard, where they carjacked a Honda Accord and a Chevy Tahoe they cut off in the drive-thru. After that they'd hit the highway, and forty minutes later they were in the Windy City.

The first thing that came to Trey's mind when he saw it was Vee calling was This bitch started all this shit. If she wouldn't have shot me, her niece wouldn't be dead, Baby Lord wouldn't be dead, Rello wouldn't dead, Flip and Dune wouldn't be in the hospital, and I wouldn't be into it with Money Gang. This bitch the devil.

He answered the call with his eyes on King Drive. Four more BDs had come outside to join them in the couple of seconds it took him to conclude that Vielle was the arsonist who'd set his whole world on fire.

"Treykwan," she said, and nothing else.

The Glock 21 in Trey's black Nike Tech pants felt unusually heavy on his hip. The .45 ACP shells were naturally heavy bullets, and the 30-round Kriss Mag-Ex2 clip was filled to capacity, but it still felt weighty. He'd buried the Glock 22 he got from Vee in Tyrisha's flower garden, and he was more than willing to turn his second Glock into another murder weapon.

He adjusted the gun and kept an eye on the passing traffic.

"Treykwan," Vee repeated. "Are you ready to talk?"

"What the fuck we got to talk about? Give me the lo on buddy ass. Tell me where Baby Gang be ducked off at. That's all I'm tryna hear right now, on David."

"Boy, I just met him —"

"You fucked that nigga! Stupid ass bitch! We got into it over that nigga, and then you went and fucked him!"

"You killed my niece, you bitch-ass nigga! Lucky I didn't fuck your brother!"

Trey clenched his teeth and growled deep in his throat. The Percocets were still working, magically reducing the ache in his shoulder to a tiny itch, but the opioid had another effect on him. It calmed his anger. Allowed him to think through his emotions.

"What the fuck did I do wrong?" he asked.

"You reached for that gun I bought you. That's what the fuck you did."

"Nah, I'm talkin' about before that. What did I do to make you go and disrespect me like that on Facebook? I fucked you good every day. Bought you clothes. Got your hair did every week damn near. What the fuck did I do?"

There was a long bout of silence from the other end. Or at least it seemed long to Trey.

Finally, Vee said, "I don't …I don't know." She paused; then: "You're right. I give you that. I was wrong for liking his pictures and all that, but you still had no right to slap me like that. Then you choked me, Trey. I was scared for my life when you did that shit."

"I just wanted you to admit who started the shit, that's all. Remember that. You started this shit. On Von, I treated you with the utmost respect all the way up until you did that bullshit. Now it's up there."

"You killed my niece, though. Let's talk about that part. How am I supposed to get over that, Treykwan? Huh? What am I…?"

Trey narrowed his eyes and looked down at his phone, suddenly realizing Vee hadn't FaceTimed him.

She always FaceTimed him.

This ho tryna set me up, he thought to himself, slowly nodding his head. He held the phone in front of his face, staring at the blank calling screen as if he could see through it and into the room where Vielle was sitting.

And where exactly was she sitting? In her living room with her police detective brother standing over her? In some office at the police station with half the Michigan City Police Department watching her and listening to their entire conversation? His thumb hovered over the "End Call " button, but he hesitated. If he hung up now, he'd have no way of knowing how much she'd already told them. On the other hand, if the police were trying to trace the call to learn his location, the way they did in all the movies, then his best move was to hang up as soon as possible.

"I ain't killed nobody," he said, very quickly. He ended the call right then, and when he looked up he saw another CPD squad car creeping past. The pig in the driver's seat — a fat-faced man with blotchy skin and dark shades — was mugging him hard.

That mug, along with Vee's suspicious phone call, was all it took for Trey to make up his mind.

The gang had plans to celebrate Rello's life with a gathering inside his sister's Parkway Gardens apartment when she made it home from work, but Trey wouldn't be there celebrating with them.

He got in the backseat of Devo's newer model Cadillac Escalade V-Series with Thirty and two more BDs, and he had Devo take him and Thirty to his baby mama Tadda Mae Cooper's house way out on 104th and Calumet, in the Roseland neighborhood. He made promises that he would return to the O before the celebrations began, but it was a lie. He gave Diana a hug and gave his seven-year-old daughter Treyquana an even bigger one, with a kiss on the cheek to sweeten the moment, and then, leaving Thirty to a box of Dunkin donuts in the kitchen, he shut off his phone and went to bed.

Chapter 20

Hard hated to do it but he transferred the money anyway, all $192,577.23 of it. He'd already handed over the $70,000 he had left in his backpack, and if he needed to he'd sell his jewelry and even his car — that sweet red Corvette he hadn't even driven yet — to get the Concord Vineyard palace he and Candy had walked through an hour earlier.

He was bone-tired when Tone Bone met up with him and Candy at a gas station near Concord Vineyard. He got out of the Durango and into Tone's matte black G-Wagon, and twenty minutes later they were in Gary, Indiana.

The Skyway into Gary was a graveyard of rusted steel and gray industry, the perfect backdrop for a gun exchange. The G-Wagon rumbled over the uneven asphalt of the industrial district, the twin-turbo V8 growling like a strong young lion.

Hard yawned in the passenger seat, his eyes fixed on the crumbling brick façade of the old steel mill. He felt the weight of the moment on his lungs, a hundred suffocating pounds of anxiety at the possibility of being busted during this pickup and sent back to the penitentiary.

"Markio a smart nigga," Tone Bone said, gripping the Alcantara steering wheel. "He said the warehouse at the end of the pier. If the feds was on us, ain't no way they would be able to see what was going on without us seeing them, too."

"Ain't no such thing as a foolproof plan."

"Markio a smart nigga," Tone repeated, as if that were the gospel.

They pulled up to a massive corrugated door that groaned open as they approached. Inside, the air was cold and smelled of grease and old dust. A crew of four black men in high-visibility construction vests and yellow hard hats were waiting. They didn't look like gangsters; they looked like men who spent their days on job sites, which was another testament to Markio's street smarts.

The men moved with practiced efficiency, rolling the three olive green wooden crates out on a hydraulic lift and loading them into the back of the G-Wagon.

Hard got out, smoking a Newport and watching them work. When they were done he stepped forward and flipped the latches on one of the crates.

The interior was lined with foam, cradling a row of pristine, short-barreled ARPs and "Hellpup" AK pistols. The second crate was even more sinister: dozens of Glocks and a small plastic bin filled with the "switches" that would turn them into handheld machine guns.

"Enough to go to war with the devil," Hard whispered, his reflection shimmering in the cold steel of a Hellpup.

Before he could close the lid, his iPhone 16 vibrated. It was Candy.

"Baby, we're here at Tamia's office," she said, her voice a sensitive mix of excitement and uncertainty. "I want that house, babe. It's perfect. But Tamia…she's being firm. She says for a 'discreet' cash closing this fast, she needs all the full amount on the table today. We gave her ninety in cash and the bank transfer went through, but we need another sixty-eight thousand and five hundred dollars. She can't hand over the keys without it. I still got the ten thousand you gave me, but we—"

"Nah, baby. You keep that," Hard said, his voice steady despite the chaos in his mind. "I'll get the money. Just give me a minute. I'll call you right back."

He hung up and stared at the crates. Tone Bone was leaning back against the G-Wagon, watching him. He'd heard enough of the conversation.

"Sixty-eight thousand?" Tone Bone said, taking a toothpick from his mouth. "That's chump change. I got that in the glove compartment and the center console right now. Go 'head and grab it. It's yours."

Hard looked at Tone Bone, his eyes narrowing into stringent slits. "What's the catch, Hard? I've known you for way too long. You ain't never just gave away no money. Not no big money."

Tone Bone became a bobblehead, his dreadlock-framed visage bobbing up and down. He walked over to Hard, and his expression turned deadly serious. "The cartel," he said. "Them Matamoros people. They're on me about the rest of the bread I owe em. I got fifty-five bricks'a girl left. My regular movers are either spooked 'cause all the beef goin' on in their hoods or too loaded up with product to buy anymore. I need you to help me sell them bricks, and all I want is thirteen thousand apiece. I need somebody with your brains, your rank, and your connections to move the last of that pack. You do that and we're clear."

Hard looked away, toward the dark waters of the lake visible through the open warehouse door. He'd told himself he was done. He'd told his P.O. he was retired. But he looked at the guns in the back of the luxury SUV, then thought of the look on Candy's face as she walked the hardwood floors in that glorious house on Riesling Court.

The 'American Dream' was expensive, and in his world, it was paid for in blood and powder.

"Just this once, Bone," Hard said, his voice sounding hard, like a cell door slamming shut. "I move them bricks and keep whatever profit I make on my end, we clear the debt, and I'm done. I'm only doing this shit for my girl."

Tone Bone smiled, a slow, knowing grin that reached his eyes. "Just this once," he echoed, both men recognizing the lie for what it was.

As they pulled away from the warehouse and started back toward Michigan City, the weight of the guns behind them was matched only by the weight of the bricks Hard knew he was about to start pushing. He was back in the game, if only for the moment, and this time if he went down he wouldn't be making it back home.

Chapter 21

There was no way HJ could focus on the Michigan Boulevard shooting with his baby sister sitting in an interrogation room two floors down.

There was also something else that had him frustrated: the questionable murder conviction that had sent his father away for two decades.

He sat back in his chair and gazed fixedly at his computer screen, biting down on his lower lip as he read the initial police report for what had to be the thousandth time this year.

After that he got up and left his office. He had other things to do — more eyewitnesses to question regarding the Michigan Boulevard shooting, more camera footage to go over in the 7th Street shooting investigation — but he could not for the life of him focus on a single thing.

"First things first," he said aloud to himself as he walked toward the staff lounge for a hot cup of coffee, his second one of the day. He needed it. Right now it felt like he was sleepwalking.

Officers Grinston, Hawkins, and Hackman were standing around the coffee machine when HJ walked in, discussing the Michigan Boulevard shooting and it's suspected ties to last night's 7th Street shooting.

"This Treykwan guy is from O Block, has it tatted across the top of his chest, and the dead guy from the Boulevard shooting had it tatted on his throat," said Officer Grinston, a thirty-year-old pretty boy with dark curly hair and skin the color of wet sand. "He even had a little necklace with 'O Block' on it. He's definitely one of Trey's boys."

"Somebody's going down over my niece getting killed," HJ interjected.

Natrisha Hawkins was black, too, an attractive little woman with a whole lot of spice in her curvy, compact frame. Brad Hackman was an older white man, tall, bespectacled, and balding with a cold stare and a snappy disposition.

The television that hung from the ceiling near the fridge was on, tuned to WSBT News because Michigan City didn't have its own news station. South Bend and Chicago stations were the usual go-to networks for Michigan City news.

Right now WSBT was giving a weather update — warmer today, but there was snow in the forecast for tonight — but every fifteen minutes or so they doubled back to the three Michigan City murders that had taken place over the span of eight hours.

Hawkins said, "I was just out there in Southgate. You know Miss Turner knows everything, so I stopped her for a word. Her grandsons hang out with Trey and his older brother. She said nobody's seen them since last night, and Big Block's daughter told her he was in the backseat of Thirty's truck when he got shot."

HJ's eyes got big. "Somebody get on the phone with St. Anthony's. We need access to their emergency room cameras. If we see Big Block getting pulled out of that Suburban, we got him on two counts of first-degree murder. Whether he was the triggerman or not."

"I'm on it," Hawkins said, and drew her department-issued smartphone.

Grinston turned to HJ. "You talked to Steiner?"

"No." HJ shook his head."Why?"

"She got a lot of information out of your sister. For one, she got her to admit that she was the one who shot Trey. She didn't confess to shooting up that Escalade, and the traffic cam right there hasn't worked in months, so we can't charge her with that one even if we wanted to. It's also looking like she shot Trey in self-defense. He practically confessed to assaulting her before she shot him."

"Wait — they actually spoke with Trey?"

Tavon Grinston offered an enthusiastic nod. "Absolutely did. Vielle called him. She accused him of slapping and choking her before she shot him, and he basically told her why he did it. She couldn't me him to confess to Journee's murder, but we don't necessarily need that. Not with what we have on Block. He'll flip. He's done it before. Twice, in fact."

"Is he still in the hospital?"

"I'll check," Hawkins said.

HJ couldn't hold back the shit-eating grin that crossed his face. Nodding, he filled a Styrofoam cup with Folgers and headed back to his office to work on getting the arrest warrant for Derrick "Big Block" Tyson.

After that he would get back to investigating the cause of his father's arrest twenty years ago, because judging from what he'd read so far, the Michigan City Police Department had some secrets of their own, and he was determined to get to the bottom of it.

Chapter 22

The O Block BDs weren't the only ones grieving.

The atmosphere inside the high-rise condo on Upper Wacker Drive was a surreal blend of extreme luxury and raw, unfiltered mourning. Through the floor-to-ceiling windows, the Chicago skyline was a cold, desolate gray, and inside, the air was warm and thick with the bittersweet scent of Wockhardt and the heavy, lingering dog of exotic bud.

This was Crystal Weatherspoon's condominium. As a top-tier Instagram model, she had turned her lethal curves and golden brown features into a half-million-dollar-a-year empire. The minimalist, white-marble aesthetic of the condo — usually reserved for brand deals and high-fashion selfies — was now the war room for Cup Gang.

In the center of the living area, Lorde sat deep in a charcoal velvet armchair. Crystal was draped across his lap, her long, dark curls spilling over his shoulders. She was breathtaking even in her grief, her black and Puerto Rican heritage showing in the sharp flare of her cheekbones and the golden undertone of her skin. She held Lorde in a desperate, crushing grip, her arms locked tight around his neck, her high-end designer loungewear — a Cashmere hoodie over matching drawstring track pants — wrinkled as she buried her face in the crook of his neck.

Nearby, Terry Lee stood like a statue near the window. He was Baby Lord's older brother, and the vacancy in his eyes was both heartbreaking and terrifying. He held a double-stacked Styrofoam cup filled with a deep purple mix of

"Wock" and peach Fanta, staring out at the city that raised him and his siblings, his mind clearly on the brother he'd just lost to a coward's drive-by.

The tension in the room was being stoked by Fayzo and Lil Luke, who were pacing the perimeter of the plush white rug like caged wolves.

"On King Neal, I'm not hearing none of that 'wait and watch and see' ass shit!" Fayzo barked, his voice echoing off the glass walls. He slammed his cup down on a glass coffee table, splashing purple drops onto a stack of high-fashion magazines. "Baby Lord was the heart of this shit! He was the prince of Baby T Blood Gang, stepped harder than anybody else from out west. They killed Lorde's daughter, Crystal's daughter, like it was nothin'. Shot Flower, shot that otha nigga. They could've killed Lorde's whole family in there last night. Chief Hard's whole family. We can't just sit back and wait, bruh. Nah. Hell nah. On Neal, a nigga gotta die behind that shit, and I ain't tryna hear shit about OTF Rello, 'cause we ain't have nothin' to do with that."

Lil Luke turned to face the room, his eyes bloodshot and blazing with a murderous energy. "We know they might be ducked off on the O. If they think bein' behind them gates make em safe. We got shit that can hit right through there. Switches and Dracos, 7.62 shells. I'm ready to slide. The fuck is we waitin' on?"

Lorde finally looked up, his expression a mask of cold, calculated stone. He didn't raise his voice, but the room went silent the moment he spoke. He took a long, slow pull off his blunt; the smoke curled around Crystal's head like a halo.

"They did that shit in Michigan City because they thought we wouldn't bring it back to the crib," Lorde said, streaming smoke out his nostrils. His voice was hard and quiet, like a stone rolling down a grassy hill. "They thought that state line was a shield. But this our city. O Block ain't had the city since King Von died and Muwop n'em got jammed up. The only Von that matter now is VonOff1700, and where shorty from? Out west, just like us. Ain't no more talkin'. We on go from here on out."

He tightened his arm around Crystal's lower back, feeling her body tremble as she sobbed against him.

"Luke, Fayz… get them Trackhawks ready," he commanded. "Terry Lee, you drink up. We goin' to O Block. If we can't catch up with Thirty or Trey, we gon' get one'a they guys."

"One?" Lil Luke smiled. "Nah. They took two of ours, we gon' take three of theirs. And that's on Baby Lord."

The million-dollar condo was silent after that, with the only soundsbeing the steady clinking of ice in Styrofoam cups and the heavy, rhythmic breathing of men with murder on their minds.

Twenty minutes later they were seated in two Jeep Grand Cherokee Trackhawks, Lorde's shiny gray one and Terry Lee's candy green one.

Destination: 64th and King Drive.

Parkway Gardens, or as it was more famously known, O Block.

Chapter 23

Katoya Jones was almost too stunning to be a prison guard. She looked more like a Victoria's Secret model, tall and slender with just enough curves to qualify her as "slim-thick." Her lips were plump and red, her hands small and feminine, and she walked like she was perpetually ripping the runway. She stepped out the back door wearing pink Von Dutch sweats and pink-and-white Air Max sneakers. The diamond on her ring finger was new to Hard; he hadn't heard anything about an engagement, but then again he'd been on the other side of the prison wall, where her outside business had nothing to do with prison politics.

Hard had a couple of Lords he'd met in prison meet him at Katoya Jones's Elston Street home and carry the crates down into her basement while he stood with her on the back porch. The young men were thuggish in appearance, with ink on their faces and necks and gold teeth in their mouths. Shamar was coal-black with braids that hung down the sides of his head like a roofline. He had a sinister smile and a notorious reputation amongst the younger generation of being a stone-cold gangster.

"You look so much better in street clothes than you did in those gray sweats," she said, beaming. "And this jewelry — I didn't know you had it like that. Who'd you get this chain from? And this watch?"

"My niggas blessed me soon's I walked out the door at ISP. That's my Corvette right there, too. Cain't lie, they looked out heavy. I just bought a crib, and I ain't even been home a full day yet."

His Corvette was parked right in front of Tone Bone's Benz truck in the alley behind Katoya's home. It was showroom-new, the gold flakes in the paint sparkling in the noontime sunshine. He had a pair of Hellpups in the trunk and two Glocks in the front of his pants. Tone Bone, who was talking on the phone in his G-Wagon, had installed the switches.

If Trey pulled up over here, he'd be in a world of trouble.

"I got some shit I need you to bring in to Bo," Hard said, trying his best to avoid eye contact with the sexy young correctional officer. He lit up a Newport and blew smoke in the wind. "All I got my hands on right now is some soft, but I'ma grab some loud from my son, too. And some of them small phones, the Jelly Pros. He can sell them for two thousand apiece all day."

"You want me to bring in some cocaine?"

He looked at her. Sometimes simple statements made him cringe, and this was one of those times.

"Don't worry, boy," she laughed. "I ain't the police. Just saying, that's a big risk. How much coke are we talking?"

"I know it's a risk, but it'll pay off, I promise. That powder goes for a hundred-a-gram all day. That's damn near three thousand off every ounce."

"How much dope am I s'posed to be bringin' in, and what's my cut?"

Hard hesitated. "Quarter brick," he said, after a lengthy bout of silence. "Nine ounces."

"Jesus Christ, Hard! That is a lotta dope." She pronounced every word clearly for emphasis. "Are you sure we can trust Bo to keep this shit on the hush? Because you know he likes to run his mouth. I ain't never heard of him snitchin' or nothin' like that, but he's always talkin' to somebody about somethin'. I ain't tryna get jammed up fuckin' with him."

"You won't. I already told him the play. You just drop off the pack and we'll see what he can do with it. I'll make sure the bros keep a tight leash on him. He'll be good."

Her bottom lip eased out over the top one, and she gave him a look. It was the same look she'd given him the night she slipped into his cell when he was serving six months in the hole. He'd fucked her on his bunk, pressing his commissary pillow down on her face to keep her screams to a minimum. He'd ejaculated in her without a second's hesitation, part of him hoping she'd come to him weeks later with pregnancy news, but the only thing she gave birth to was the taped-up package of Suboxone strips and tobacco he had her bring in a few days later.

"You still with that Candy girl who always came up there to visit you?"

He gave a small nod, which made one corner of Katoya's upper lip curl in disgust. She rolled her eyes and made a "mm" sound in her throat.

"I might send my son or one of his guys over here to grab a few of them guns," he said, to change the subject. "If it ain't him, and if you don't get a call from me, don't let nobody else in that basement. And if you let Shamar come back back over here keep him outta that basement."

Katoya rolled her eyes at Hard and smiled. "Boy, you need to stop. I ain't even let my man come over here yet, and he proposed to me the other day." She held up her left hand to show him the ring he'd already seen. "See?"

"Who's the lucky man?"

"Lieutenant Erickson. You know he the husband type. I put this pussy on his old ass and he bought me a ring three weeks later."

Hard knew Lieutenant Erickson. He was an older man from somewhere in Ohio. He ran A-Cell House at ISP, and for awhile back in the day he'd been a mule just like his new fiancée. Hard had paid him $5,000 for two moves, both of which had been three ounces of heroin and two cell phones.

Hard had cleared over seventy thousand dollars off those two moves.

"Congratulations," Hard said to Katoya as he did his gang's handshake with his two helpers, Keezy and Shamar. They had just walked out the back door.

He'd given Keezy a Glock 19 and Shamar a Glock 23, both with extended magazines.

"The fuck you got in them boxes?" Keezy asked.

For this Shamar gave him a sharp smack across the back of his braided head. Katoya yelped a laugh and Hard chuckled, and the two young Vice Lords stumbled down the porch steps playfully throwing fists at each other. Shamar turned around and blew Katoya a kiss before he headed out the back gate; she blushed and waved goodbye to him and his friend.

"That's crazy how you can just call them boys over here to do what you ask them to do. People around here are scared to even say their names. Shamar, that black some bitch just shot a nigga eight times out there on Pleasant Ave. They got it on camera and everything."

Katoya's sweet North Carolina accent came through loud and clear. She was from Rocky Mount, a country girl whose mother had come to Chicago chasing a dream. When that dream didn't pan out, Mama Jones detoured to Michigan City on the heels of a Chicago man who'd impregnated her with her one and only child. He got killed in Gary, Indiana — drug deal gone wrong— and Katoya grew up to be an Indiana DOC guard at the age of twenty-one. Hard had met her on her second month of work, when the administration moved her to the segregation unit to keep her away from the thirsty young savages in general population. The plan was technically a failure, since the cameras in seg didn't work, leaving an opening for her to slip into Hard's cell in the middle of the night, where he'd fucked the living daylights out of her. After her shift was over and she was home comfortable in bed, he'd FaceTimed her and listened to the aforementioned history of the Jones clan. When Hard told her that his own mother was also originally from North Carolina — Mama Gaing hailed from Princeville, "the oldest town incorporated by African Americans in the United States," as Mama was so fond of saying— he and Katoya had formed a special bond that made him feel good about helping paying off her house and her swampy green 2024 Jeep Wrangler.

Over the span of eighteen months, he'd given her a little over $60,000.

A passing wind blew a whiff of Katoya's designer perfume in Hard's direction, stiffening a phallus that belonged to Tazera Williams.

At least he wanted it to belong to Tazera. Right now it was, quite literally, leaning toward Katoya.

She sighed and leaned her shoulder against his elbow. Then her arm went around him, and she said, "I'll break off the engagement. All you gotta do is say the word."

Hard wagged his head and said nothing.

"You know I've always wanted to be with you," Katoya went on. "Ain't no nigga ever looked out for me and my daughter the way you have. I mean ever. Her daddy ain't gave me a dime in years. You're the reason she never goes without. I mean, my paycheck and the DOC benefits are okay, but we have a paid off house because of the money I got from you. I'm only twenty-three. What other twenty-three-year-old you know own a house? I'm winnin' because'a you, big daddy."

Hard gave her a caring squeeze and was glad when Tone Bone leaned out his window and shouted, "Bruh, we got shit to do. Come on, man! I'm hungry as a hostage."

With a deep chuckle and a heartfelt goodbye, Hard left Katoya standing there on the porch and started down the wet porch steps.

There was hardly any snow left on the ground, but all the grass and dirt was muddy, so Hard walked carefully up the redbrick walkway to the chain-link gate.

"When you gon' come by with the stuff for Bo?" Katoya shouted after him.

"Soon's I get it," Hard shouted back. He looked at her and saw her smile a sexy, suggestive smile. She interlaced her fingers under her chin, like a woman in prayer.

Tone said, "About time. Damn. Felt like I was watchin' a scene from The Young and the Restless. Ol' lovey-dovey ass shit."

Katoya cracked up laughing on the porch and turned to head inside just as her six-year-old daughter, Lynnie, appeared in the doorway, a pretty little brown girl in blue jeans and a salmon-colored sweater with some sort of design on the chest. Her hair was done in a dizzying maze of cornrows that ended in colorful beads. She showed a gap-toothed smile and waved at Hard as he opened the driver's door of his Corvette. He waved back and watched Katoya hustle Lynnie back inside, then he turned and gave his sweet chariot another longing look before he lowered himself into the driver's seat.

The car was a true beauty, and he was glad he'd taken the time to stop by Vee's house and get it before heading over to Katoya's place.

It was the paint that got him: a shiny candy apple red over a radiant gold base. In the shade it looked like a deep, dark cherry, but when the Indiana sun hit struck those curves it changed, the gold flakes waking up, making the paint look like shifting, molten lava. It had a wet look to it, as if the clear coat was still dripping.

The body featured the ZTK Performance Package, which added a massive, visible carbon-fiber high-wing spoiler and a front splitter that threatened every curb in Michigan City. It rolled on staggered 20-inch front and 21-inch rear visible carbon-fiber wheels with a thin red pinstripe around the rim.

Tucked behind them were big Brembo brakes with calipers painted to match the gold flakes in the body.

The interior has the highest-tier 3LZ trim and was customized to feel more like a private jet than a car. There was a 14-inch digital gauge cluster for the driver, a 12.7-inch infotainment screen, and a 6.6-inch auxiliary touchscreen to the left of the steering wheel just for performance stats. Every inch of the jet black interior was wrapped in Nappa leather and sueded microfiber. The GT2 racing seats had carbon-fiber halos and custom red stitching.

And there was more.

The removable electrochromic roof panel could change from 100% transparent to opaque with the touch of a button. The 14-speaker Bose Performance System was stupendously loud, as Hard had learned as soon as he started his old school rap playlist and UGK's "Pocket Full of Stones" began blaring from all those speakers.

Hard sat back in the seat and got himself situated, putting one Glock under his right thigh and the other one under his left one; he didn't want to have to wrestle the guns out of his pants if Trey happened to pull up next to him in traffic.

When he started the engine, pressing the Z Mode button on the steering wheel and beaming as the exhaust valves snapped open, turning the quiet cruiser into a street weapon that vibrated the windows of every house on the block.

A Bluetooth call came through from Tone Bone before he could even get his music playlist going.

"Yeah," Hard answered.

"Boaaaaa! That engine! Damn! I know you feel like the king of the world in that pretty muhfucka. You gon' have to let me drive that. I'll trade you the Wagon for a couple days."

"Maybe later."

"Later? Damn, big homie. I thought we was better than that." He laughed, a belly-deep sound that dragged another tired smile out of Hard. "Nah, but listen: we need to be gettin' them straps to Lorde n'em. They gon' need em to go at Trey and the rest of them BDs. They say twelve found some'n like a hun'ed eighty shells out there by that GoLo. Some boy named Shaggy got shot up pretty bad."

"I ain't even heard from Lorde. Let me hit him right quick. I'll call you back. Follow me back to La Porte. I gotta drop that money off to Candy."

"Nah, I'm about to go grab them bricks. Already got em out here, just gotta ride out there to Southgate to get em."

Hard paused. A part of him wanted to give Tone Bone's money and turn down those fifty-five bricks. That was the part of him that never wanted to see the inside of a prison cell again. But the part of him was foolish — it had to be foolish — because what man in his right mind would risk going back when he'd been innocent of the charges to begin with?

A vengeful man, that's who. A man who'd seen his son's daughter die right before his eyes. A man who was determined to take care of his family and protect them by any means necessary, even if it meant buying a house he could barely even afford so that his family could have a safe, out-of-the-way place to lay their heads.

That man was the old Hard, the real Hard, and that man had taken over Hard's mindset.

He tried calling Lorde and got no answer. After that he veered around Tone Bone's G-Wagon and shot off down the Elston Street alleyway, on his way back to La Porte.

Chapter 24

Lorde didn't answer because he'd turned off his phone the minute he hopped in his Trackhawk with Fayzo and Lil Luke. Terry Lee was behind them in his green one, and they were slicing through early afternoon traffic on the Dan Ryan, en route to Parkway Gardens.

"Hold fast," Luke said, holding up his iPhone in the passenger seat. He was the only member who'd kept his phone turned on, and that was only because he had a groupie on his dick who just so happened to be one of OTF Maeski's favorite TikTok models. Her given name was Gabrielle Crocker, but she was more famously known as Trench Doll. She had guns and gang signs tatted on her. She had her nose, ears, nipples, and clitoris pierced, and sometimes she posted photos in sexy designer bikinis and lacy Fenty lingerie.

"Give me five thousand and I'll tell you where they at right now," she said. "Just make sure it don't get out where you got the lo from. I can't afford to die over this shit. I got mouths to feed. Two kids, my sister, my mama. You know how this shit go."

Lil Luke looked at Lorde, the undisputed breadwinner of their crew. Just two nights ago he'd sold out the Aragon Ballroom in Uptown, performing on stage in front of five thousand people, and at the end of the night he'd cleared $20,000. That same night he'd performed at another sold-out show at The Riviera Theater that brought in an additional $25,000. He was fast becoming one of the city's go-to artists for drill music. Combine the rap money with the tens of thousands he made selling weed and you had one hell of a money machine.

"I got it," he said to Lil Luke. He took an obnoxiously thick pile of hundred-dollar bills out of his pants pocket — $20,000 cash — and told Luke to "Count out that nickel."

Trench Doll was live on FaceTime. She was all big eyes and teeth watching Lil Luke thumb through those racks. By the time he got to five thousand she'd already given up the address: the celebrations for OTF Rello had started in Parkway Gardens and moved on to The Gold Room in Stone Park, just west of the city near O'Hare. Devo was there with around twenty other BDs. Thirty and Trey weren't there yet, but Devo had told Trench Doll that Trey was supposed to be pulling up. They were in the VIP section, throwing dollars and popping bottles at four o'clock in the afternoon.

"Y'all can sit back or some'n, wait for them niggas to get there. You'll know it's him when you see him. His arm's in a blue sling from a gunshot wound." She went quiet for a couple of seconds; then: "Was it one'a y'all who shot him in the shoulder?"

"My lil sister shot that nigga," Lorde said, cackling. "He got shot by a female and did a drive-by on her house as get back. Killed a lil girl."

He didn't mention that the little girl was his daughter. He thought that admission would have broken him, and on top of that it could lead the police right to him if word got back to the authorities.

But it was too late. Trench Doll already knew. "I saw it on Kollege Kidd. They said it was Rap Lorde's daughter." She paused then added, "That sounded like Rap Lorde I was just talkin' to."

Lorde reached over and pressed the End Call button. They already had the location. The Gold Room was one of his favorite strip clubs, right up there with Redbone's and Queen of Diamonds. In fact, it was a paid appearance at The Gold Room that had first allowed him to lay eyes on Crystal. He'd seen her in the VIP section with some of her famous model friends — a whole crew of baddies — but it was Crystal who'd caught his eye, her sexy smile and all that ass she naturally possessed.

Now the daughter he'd given her was dead, killed by a coward's bullet.

For that there would be hell to pay.

Lorde detoured and jumped on the Eisenhower Expressway (I-290 West), which was the quickest route to The Gold Room. He had Fayzo phone Terry Lee with the change of plans, and then he pressed play on "Walkin' in Blood," a record he'd recently dropped that featured Screwly G and Bloodhound Q50. The song was released just five weeks ago and it already had over two million views on YouTube:

"I caught a opp on North Ave, upped sword fast and I hawked em

Then twelve came, did some lookin' 'round, got a chalk stick and just chalked em

Rap Lorde walked through so much blood that it left stains on his shoe soles

He got two poles wit' so many bodies on em he nicknamed em Glock Coffins…"

Lorde really had caught an opp on North Avenue, a stick-thin dreadhead named Kaneef Edwards who'd been more famously known as SplattaBoy. He felt comfortable speaking on that unsolved homicide in his music because he'd done it with Baby Lord and Terry Lee, two notorious killers who'd been doing it for years without a single felony conviction.

This evening he would be walking in blood for Baby Lord, and he wasn't going home until either Trey or someone close to him was dead.

"Trench Doll ain't gon' say shit," Lil Luke said, setting Trench Doll's five grand to the side and handing the remaining pile of hundreds back to Lorde. "She the backdoor queen, and she ain't liked Trey ever since he robbed her cousin a few years ago. Remember when Dre from Lamron got poked for his jewelry."

Lorde shrugged. His mind had already raced past the issue of Trench Doll possibly knowing too much. All he wanted to do now was take a long, angry walk through Trey's blood; he had an almost vampiric thirst for that man's blood, and he wasn't going home until that thirst was quenched.

Chapter 25

After Hard took the $68,500 to Candy at Tamia's La Porte office he counted through what was left and saw that he had $4,300. More than enough to pay for a really nice lunch with his lady; not nearly enough to get any furniture for their newly acquired home.

He followed her Durango from Tamia's office to Trattoria Enzo on Michigan Avenue. It was the kind of place that felt tucked away and established — warm lighting, white tablecloths, and the homely scent of garlic and simmering marinara drifting in the air.

Tamia had recommended it as "the place where the city's power players eat," and Hard liked the vibe immediately. It was quiet enough for a conversation and upscale enough that nobody was going to start trouble. They sat in a corner booth, tucked into the shadows. Hard ordered the Filet Mignon, medium rare, and a glass of the darkest red wine on the menu. Candy leaned across the table, her smile fading into something serious, looking at him with eyes that were half-terrified and half-thrilled.

"You really just dropped all that money on a place for us," she whispered, her voice trembling. "That house…it's like a castle."

"And I want you to move in with me. You can find a job somewhere out here. Your daughter's, what, nineteen now? She can just stay living with your brother at that house in Avon. We ain't gon' have to pay nothin' but utilities and property taxes here, so keeping up the mortgage down there shouldn't be a problem."

Candy took his big left hand in both of hers and squeezed. Her eyes filled with tears. Hard reached across the table and thumbed those tears away.

"What did I tell you last week?" Hard said. "When I get out, just give me some time. I'm gon' make sure we're straight. This just the start of it, baby. I ain't gon' let what happened last night fuck up what we had planned. We're good, you hear me? We're good."

"I…I love you, Hard." She laughed at something and said, "I love you hard, Hard. I swear to God I do."

"And I love you even more."

He leaned across the table and kissed her on the mouth, a slow, sensual kiss that sent more tears flowing down her dimpled cheeks.

"Hurry up and eat," Hard said, digging into his meal. "We gotta get back to Michigan City and grab us a hotel room for the night. I'm tired as hell."

They talked a bit while they ate. Candy's daughter, Tayda, owned a cleaning service in Indianapolis, and she was starting to reap the benefits of being a CEO at nineteen. Last month she'd taken home twelve grand. She was also a college sophomore with a good-for-nothing boyfriend who was always borrowing money he couldn't pay back.

Candy's older brother, Tyrik, was a former MMA fighter who was currently unemployed and living off his sister and niece. He had a Dodge Challenger Hellcat that was his pride and joy. He used it to get the girls and occasionally to make a few bucks driving for Uber. Candy loved him too much to ask for any help with the rent, but she didn't mind complaining about it to Hard.

Candy didn't stop talking about her family until they were done eating. They left the restaurant after that, and Hard trailed her from the La Porte restaurant the Blue Chip Casino in Michigan City. Hard spent most of the twenty-minute drive on the phone with Vee, who'd just been released from police custody.

"HJ arrested me, Daddy," she cried. "They had me in a fuckin' interrogation room, askin' me all kinda questions about Trey. Some cop named Steiner did all the questioning. She had me thinking I was cooked."

"And you say HJ arrested you?"

"Mmm hmm. Caught me walkin' up the alley behind Bambi's house and pulled right up on me. They took my gun for evidence over me shooting Trey. He had told them that it was me who started all the drama with him the night before you got out. Made it seem like I just upped and shot him, like he hadn't slapped me and choked the fuck outta me. I tried to get him to confess to killing Journee in front of that cop but he hung up on me. They let me go after that. All charges dismissed. HJ had the nerve to demand a thank you, like he did me a favor or some'n. Arresting me and taking my gun ain't favor. Had me in there scared outta my mind, so scared I tried to set a nigga up to get outta there."

"Don't ever do that again, baby girl. We don't work for the police. You let them do their job. Only thing you should say when they're tryna question you is 'I want to speak with my with my lawyer,' and nothing else. You got that?"

Vielle said she did.

"I just bought a house," Hard said. "A real nice one. It's on the North side of La Porte, in Concord Vineyard."

"I ain't never even heard of that."

"I hadn't, either. Don't tell nobody the address to that house. Flower and Lorde can know, but that's it. Keep it to yourself. I should be moving in within the next day or two, and you know you're welcome to move in with me any time you feel like it. I really wanna demand that you move in with me at least for the first couple of days, but you're a grown woman, way too old for me to be telling you what to do, so I'll leave that up to you."

"No, I'm staying in my own house. Not to say I wouldn't appreciate a room there too, but I ain't lettin' nobody run me out my house. Damn that. I just went and bought me a whole new gun, a Glock 21. I'm ready for whatever."

"Where you at now?"

"On the road with Bambi and Kela."

"And me!" Tonya shouted. "Don't forget about little ol' me!"

Hard chuckled his amusement. Tonya had been flirting with him ever since she first glimpsed him on a FaceTime call with Vee. He always told her she was too young, and that he wouldn't dare mess around with one of his baby girl's friends, but the truth was, under the right circumstances, and if he wasn't in a committed relationship with Candy, Tonya could get it. She was a bad, caramel-hued, eighteen-year-old stunner who was thick in all the right places and had just enough jiggle in her step to drive a man insane.

"They just picked me up from the police station. We're about to go back to the house on 7th Street—"

"I don't want you over there, baby girl. Not without me."

"I'll be fine, Daddy." Vielle didn't sound so sure of herself when she said it. "I'm just pickin' up some clothes and stuff. I'll be stayin' with Bambi for the next day or two, but I ain't movin' outta my house."

Hard thought it over. "Okay, fine — but hurry up. Get in there, grab what you need, and get out. And text me when you leave so I know you're okay."

"Okay. Love you, Daddy. I'll text you."

Hard turned on some rap music and drove. He wanted to call HJ and check him about arresting his own sister, he wanted to go to the west side of Michigan City to make sure Vee was safe while she grabbed her things from inside last night's crime scene, but truthfully he was too exhausted to do any of that. He needed a bed. He needed five or six hours of good, comfortable sleep. Everything else would have to wait.

Chapter 26

Candy didn't want to go back to Vielle's house either, not with all the yellow tape and bullet holes in the siding. She needed somewhere with security, cameras, and a door that locked with an electronic click.

So she was glad when Hard led her to Michigan City's Blue Chip Casino Hotel & Spa.

Hard didn't go for a standard room. He walked right up to the desk in the Spa Blu Tower and paid cash for one of the high-floor suites.

The room was massive, with floor-to-ceiling windows that looked out over a frozen Lake Michigan and the lights of the city. The carpet was thick, and the king-size bed was wrapped in high-thread-count linen that had to feel like heaven compared to the thin, scratchy wool blankets Hard had slept under for the past twenty years.

When Candy came out of the bathroom from showering and changing into a black silk pair of pajamas (the bottoms were short-shorts, and the top was a small, short-sleeved button-up), she found Hard standing at the window, watching the snow swirl against the glass. The amber liquor in his glass was undoubtedly cognac, and as she walked up behind him and wrapped him in her arms, snaking her hands under his white Sinew T-shirt. She could almost feel the weight of the last twenty years weighing down on him, and as they looked out at the Indiana shoreline, she thought she could sense something else, too: homesickness.

"You miss Chicago, don't you?" she asked, her voice barely audible over the soft R&B music she'd left playing in the bedroom.

"Of course I miss Chicago. The Italian beef sandwiches. The block parties. The footworkin' and the drug money, the gangbangin' and the lingo. What respected man wouldn't miss his own city, especially if that city is my city? I love Chicago. I know people think it's dangerous, and it is for certain people, but I'm not one of those people. You're safe with me, I promise. Anywhere we go, from Chicago to here, you're safe. That thing last night was just a fluke. That's the first time my family's ever come under fire, and Trey is going to die about that. Thirty, too. They crossed a line that can't be uncrossed." He shook his head. "That's final."

Candy didn't say anything for several minutes after that. She let her fingers do the talking, tracing the valleys between Hard's six-pack as the two of them stood there at the floor-to-ceiling window, staring out at the vast expanse of Lake Michigan. It looked like a sheet of hammered steel, with white-capped waves and jagged shelves of ice building up along the shore. They could see the Michigan City East Pierhead Lighthouse standing out in the water, encased in a layer of ice that made it look like a frozen statue. Looking west they could see the white, snow-covered peaks of the Indiana Dunes.

"Get comfortable, Candy," Hard said, not turning around. "We ain't never goin' back to the trenches. From here on out, we live like this."

That was when he turned around. He placed a hand on her hip and gazed into her eyes, licking his lips and giving an expression that bordered on a grin. That big hand moved behind her and she felt the fingers dig into the meaty flesh of her ass, squeezing and rubbing. Candy leaned in to plant a kiss on the shimmering diamond "HARD" pendant attached to his Cuban-link necklace, and Hard lowered his head to plant his kiss on her mouth. The smooch became two kisses, three, and then it went French.

She tasted the liquor on his breath. Felt the thick, eleven-inch length of muscle in his sweatpants growing harder and longer, like an inflating balloon. He swallowed down the last inch of liquor in his glass and kissed her again, even more passionately than before. She took the empty glass and he picked her up, letting her wrap her legs around his waist.

"Let's go to bed for a little while," she said, and getting some rest was the furthest thing from her mind.

Hard smacked her on the ass and began the slow, deliberate walk across the room. His white-on-white Air Force Ones made no sound on the heavy carpet, his hair steady and confident — the walk of a man who knew what he was doing.

"You ain't goin' back to Nap for at least a week," he murmured, his voice a low rumble against her skin.

"I don't want to be anywhere else," she whispered back, burying her face into the crook of his neck.

The icy Cuban links of his chain were cold against her collarbone, a sharp contrast to the heat radiating from him. He reached the edge of the king-size bed and paused for a beat, looking down at her in the dim light of the room. The sprawling view of the shoreline was behind them now, replaced by the quiet, high-end luxury of the tower. He leaned forward, lowering her onto the cool white linens, his eyes never leaving hers.

"I know you're tired," Candy said, setting the glass next to her on the foot-end of the bed, "but we didn't really get to finish what we started last night."

"We gon' finish that right now."

Hard gave her shorts a sharp yank that sent the silky fabric sliding down her sumptuous legs. Once he had the shorts off he pushed her long legs up and lowered his head between her parted thighs.

The first sucky kiss on the hood of her clitoris made Candy gasp and shudder. She put her hands flat on the back of his bald head, holding in that gasp of breath as his tongue delved between her slippery vaginal lips and slid up to her clitoris, where he spent a few minutes licking and sucking while his hands caressed her hips and thighs.

Her toes curled over so tightly that several of the knuckles popped. She made a high-pitched noise in her throat and tried sliding away from himbut he held on, locking his arms around her thighs.

Tazera was proud of herself. She'd been faithful to Hard for the majority of their five-year relationship. Sure, there were a couple of nights when she'd gone out to the bar with her friend Kiara and gone home with some random man — a Nigerian goldsmith who'd turned out to be an extreme cheapskate, and a Ben Davis high school football coach who'd promised to give her the world if she could only stop communicating with her incarcerated lover. Other than that, the only man she'd slept with was EJ, an ugly black boy from Indianapolis's Haughville neighborhood with a mouthful of gold teeth and a stack of shoe boxes full of drug money. She hadn't been with him in three or four months, but he was always messaging her on Instagram and sending her money on Cash App. He'd paid for the plane tickets for her and her daughter to fly out to New York City for an NBA Youngboy concert at the Barclay's Center late last September, and he'd also helped Candy pay off some school loans, both for herself and her daughter, who was currently a sophomore at Butler University. EJ ate pussy like a meat-starved carnivore, and he had some really good dick, but Candy had no plans of ever letting him back into her bed. Not with Hard home.

She wondered how EJ would feel about that.

It must have been the incredible tongue-lashing Hard was giving her that had her thinking about EJ. Hard was pretty good at it himself. Great, actually. In less than ten minutes he had her screaming out in orgasm, and before she could recover he shoved her legs up and sunk his nearly-foot-long elephant trunk right into her, stretching her deep and wide.

"Ooouuu," Candy moaned as she took his face in her hands and kissed his glossy-wet lips, tasting herself in the kiss and liking it. "I love you, Har…Har…" His name became an ear-piercing moan.

Hard dug in deeper with every forward thrust of his powerful hips. He pushed her pajama top up over her naked breasts and pinched her left nipple between his thumb and forefinger.

"You so fuckin' sexy," he said, rotating that pinched nipple as he continued to glide his dick in and out of her.

She looked down at his huge black penetrating snake and wondered how such a behemoth could fit in her tight little pussyhole. Hard put a finger in her mouth and she immediately began sucking it — sucking it the way she wanted to suck his dick, swirling her tongue around the second knuckle and staring at the pendant dangling from his necklace.

HARD.

His name fit him like his T-shirt, which had SINEW emblazoned across the left chest area. His sweatpants had the same word on the left pantleg. Candy had never heard of Sinew, but she loved the their clothes fit on her man.

Although she thought he'd look even better not wearing anything at all.

"Take off…your shirt," she said in between moans.

Hard leaned back and pulled the T-shirt over his head. Candy gawked at all the concrete slabs of muscle he had in his chest, arms, and abdomen. Even his shoulders bulged with muscle, hard and unyielding.

Meanwhile, her favorite muscle of his kept sliding in and out of her, rearranging her organs. She could feel her juices gathering around the girth of his dick and dribbling down over her butthole. His sweatpants and boxers were down around his knees, his twin Glocks right next to him on the bed.

Candy's eyeballs rolled up in their sockets from the supreme dickdown she was receiving. She'd fucked some well-endowed men in the past, but had any of them been packing like Hardis Gaing Senior? Absolutely not. The biggest she'd had before Hard was a ten-incher, from an Army sergeant in Detroit, Michigan, and his sex game didn't have shit on the way Hard was fucking her. She had tears in her eyes, which were still rolled upward, and her mouth had been agape for the past five minutes.

He worked his hips like Hebrew slaves, long-stroking her, short-stroking her, fucking her senseless. She rotated her fingertips on her rigid clitoris for a couple of minutes and then she came again, moaning and shoving at his chest to push him away.

Candy might as well have been pushing on a solid brick wall. Hard didn't budge an inch. He was like a steel machine wrapped in human muscle and skin, a living, breathing sex monster. She looked up at him with her eyes wide and her mouth hanging open.

"Yeah. Yeeeeeah," Hard said, really feeling himself. He lowered his head to suck on her nipple, the one he'd pinched. "Mmm hmm. I told you what was gon' happen when they let me out that cage, didn't I? I don't know why you thought it was a game."

Candy wanted to reply, say something like "Don't flatter yourself," but she couldn't form a single word. His dick has effectively silenced her.

Fifteen minutes of missionary and Hard flipped her over and positioned her so that her back was arched, her head was down, and her fat round ass was raised high in front of him.

He took two steps back from the bed, and when Candy looked back over her shoulder she thought he was merely taking a moment to admire the view. He was really just stepping out of his sweatpants and boxer briefs. He took off his shoes, too, and returned to bed wearing nothing but his chain and watch.

Candy had always wondered what it would be like to fuck an athlete. She felt like that dream was coming true, despite the fact that Hard had never gone pro. At 6'-5" he was the absolute tallest man she'd ever dated, and he was strong as an ox, so overly stuffed with muscles that a bullet might have trouble getting all the way through him.

He got up on the bed and kneeled behind her, smacking his dick on her jiggly buttocks and giving each cheek a good hard smack.

"I'm finna try to break yo' back," Hard informed her.

Beaming, Candy wiggled her generous hips. Hard spread her butt cheeks apart and guided his missile into her silo.

"Mmmmm," Candy cried.

"Shut the fuck up. Shut up and take this dick. It's what you asked for, what you been waitin' five years for. And I'ma give it to you."

Hard started fucking her. Before long she was screaming into the snow-white comforter, feeling his hands on her waist and his dick in her guts. There was a saying among women — "It hurt so good!" — but Candy had never fully understood it until now. She balled her hands into fists and endured a pain that felt soooo good.

The Concord Vineyard house came to her mind. She imagined herself getting fucked like this for years on end in that amazingly beautiful home, walking around half-naked while her man sat playing the game or watching the game on a huge living room TV, decorating the many rooms for the holidays, having cookouts and family gatherings on that half-acre back lawn.

She opened her eyes and throat and let out a ululating scream as a third orgasm tore through her.

"I'm comin', too," Hard said, pulling out of her and stroking himself over her still-wobbling ass.

Candy felt the cum splashing across her bountiful derriere. She looked back to see the gusher and caught a splat right in the eye. The rest of that stream landed across the back and shoulder of her pajama top, a long strip of semen that had the look and consistency of thick white snot.

More jets of Hard's baby batter shot out of him as he continued to pump his dick over her ass. It was still spouting when he slipped back into her and pushed forward, cramming his gushing phallus inside of her.

"Why'd you pull out if you was just gon' finish inside of me?" Candy asked.

It was a question Hard had no answer for. He smacked his deflating member on her cum-splattered ass, beaming a thousand-watt smile.

"We gon' have a whole lotta fun together," he said, nodding his head in agreement with his own declaration.

If dicking her down like he just had was Hard's idea of fun, then Candy was all in.

Chapter 27

The JKS recycling lot at 3800 West Lake Street was the perfect spot to sit and watch the front entrance to The Gold Room. It was directly across the street. Lorde was a known face in the city, and he knew that the club owners would immediately recognize him if he pulled up to the valet-only strip club. The DJ would announce his arrival if he decided to step inside the club, so he chose the smarter option and pulled into the unfenced JKS Ventures parking lot across the street. From there he had a panoramic view of The Gold Room's entrance without being caught in the glare of the valet lights.

It was just after eight o'clock and Lorde had been parked there for over two hours, watching and waiting. His sleek gray Trackhawk was a ghost in the dark, its flat primer-grey paint seeming to soak up the industrial yellow street lights. Next to his Jeep, Terry Lee's Trackhawk was a shadow, visible only when the light hit the yellow brake calipers peeking through spokes.

They weren't idling anymore. The engines were off, but the heat still rippled off the vented hoods, making the air shimmer. Inside the Jeeps, the only light was the dull green glow of the dashboards and the occasional spark of a lighter.

"I can't wait to see this nigga pull up, gang," Fayzo said from the backseat. "I'm knockin' his whole face off. Up close and personal, on me. Bet they remember this!"

Lorde toked on his blunt and stared across the street at The Gold Room, thinking about the show he'd done at the

Aragon. It was one of his favorite shows, mostly because of the special guest appearance from MBM's Young Meach, one of his favorite Midwest rappers. YM was a ranking member of the Four Corner Hustlers with ridiculously long money. A four-time Grammy Award winner, he'd been a successful rap artist for more than a decade now, pushing out hit after hit with Money Bagz Management's billionaire CEO, Blake "Bulletface" King, and dozens of other top-tier artists. He was featured on "Can't Go," another one of Lorde's hit records off his Lorde of the Streets mixtape, and he was also Lorde's plug for the bales of exotic bud he'd made so much money off of, money he'd used to take Journee to Disney World, to pay for her private homeschooling, to buy her everything she'd ever wanted and more.

Journee was gone now, shot dead in her Aunt Vee's dining room.

Lorde gripped the handle of his Micro Draco and sneered at an enemy who hadn't yet arrived.

"I'm on the same shit, bruh," Lorde said to Fayzo. "I cain't fuckin' wait for this nigga to pull up."

Chapter 28

Trey dipped his pinkie nail into the small baggie of cocaine and made the mini mountain of snow disappear up his left nostril.

"Yo' dope fiend ass," Thirty said, looking up from his phone.

"Gotta stay up and on point tonight, folks," Trey replied. "This shit gon' keep me on my square, make me so paranoid I'm watchin' everything."

The two brothers were in the backseat of an Uber, a burnt orange Hyundai Santa Fe. The driver was black like them, a forty-something man with short curly hair and a huge black birthmark on his left cheek. He was playing an old Crucial Conflict song over the stereo system, smoking a Newport 100, and bobbing his head to the beat.

They were about fifteen minutes into the thirty-five-minute ride from 104th and Calumet to The Gold Room in Stone Park, coasting down I-290 West on a chilly winter evening in Chicago.

"Tierra gon' meet us there in my Maybach," Thirty said. He was texting her on WhatsApp. "She bringin' my jewelry, too. I told her to bring that bussdown AP and that O Block chain for you. That way you'll at least have some "j" on when we walk in there."

"I don't need no jewelry on, nigga. You see this outfit? I'm the freshest nigga in the party off the rip."

"Maybe the second freshest." Thirty popped the collar on his gray-and-blue Dior Oblique Wool Jacquard sweater. His sweatpants matched the top, and so did his Dior running shoes. "This a seven-thousand-dollar fit, li'l nigga. You ain't on shit."

Of course Thirty was only kidding. Trey was Burberry from head to toe, with the top being a bubbly black diamond-quilted nylon bomber jacket over a relaxed cotton flannel, his pants being check twill trousers, and his shoes being the brand's check terrace leather sneakers — a $4,500 getup. He had his .45-caliber Glock in the inner pocket of his bomber jacket, $5,700 in cash in his pocket, and a madman's glare in his eyes.

Trey spent a few minutes watching live video from inside The Gold Room — on Devo and Dank's Instagram pages, Maeski's Snapchat, and Trench Doll's Facebook page.

Devo and the gang were in one of the ultra-exclusive Champagne Rooms, private areas where all the high-rollers went for bottle service away from the main floor. Someone had already gotten a bunch of RIP OTF Rello shirts made; how they'd managed to do that so soon after Rello's death was a mystery to Trey. He counted at least fifteen certified gang members in the background of Devo's videos. Trey nodded his head and smiled, proud of his gang for showing up in support of OTF Rello.

It was Trench Doll's live video that really made Trey want to join the celebrations. She and her girls were turnt in the Skybox section, shaking ass and throwing ones. Trench Doll was a snake — everybody in Parkway Gardens knew it — but there was no denying her beauty. She was a brown-skinned baddie with tattoos from her face and neck way down to her feet, and she was always with a squad of equally attractive young thotties, hood bitches who'd do anything under the sun for a designer purse and a five-hundred-dollar wig. This evening she was with Sahara, Danielle, Megan, and a famous Chicago stripper/porn star nicknamed BunnyXXX.

"On King David, I'm in that bitch," Trey said, leaving a few fire emojis under Trench Doll's video. "I been tryna fuck on Trench Doll ever since she got that BBL, gang. Shorty so thick now. You saw her in that 42 Dugg video. She know how to make that fat muhfucka do tricks."

"That bitch hate you, bruh. The fuck you mean you tryna fuck her? Youpoked one'a her people."

Trey shrugged one shoulder and nearly jumped in his seat when Trench Doll replied to his flame emojis with a kiss emoji. She also "loved" his comment.

"Look." He showed Thirty the exchange. "This ho on my dick."

He decided to go live on Instagram to show off his outfit. Diana had bought it for him with the profits she made from helping Thirty get off his loads of exotic bud. She had just paid Thirty the seven thousand dollars she owed him from the last load he'd dumped on her, and she still had a couple of pounds to herself.

Trey took out his cash and spread it out across his lap before going live with a selfie video that instantly began gaining traction. People in Michigan City who knew him started commenting with "boom" and "wow" emojis, while his fellow Chicagoans complimented him on his fit and his bankroll. He had twenty-eight thousand followers, mostly because of his longtime affiliation with OTF. He'd grown up around all of O Block's drill rap legends, from Sosa to Von and everyone in between. They'd gone to the same Englewood schools, fucked on the same Englewood thotties, and shot at the same Englewood opps, often with the same guns. His Instagram page was a vast collection of photos and videos of him with some of his gang's most outstanding members, which gained him more and more followers every day.

The Uber driver's playlist was perfect for Trey's live video. Crucial Conflict segued into Chief Keef's "Kobe," and Screwly G came on after that.

At least Trey thought it was Screwly. He was panning the camera down to his shoes when he realized that the song he was listening to was Rap Lorde's "Walkin' in Blood," and as soon as it registered his arrogant grin became a petulant scowl.

"Turn this weak-ass shit off," he said, loud enough for the driver to hear. When the song kept playing Trey fixed his mouth to repeat his demand, but his phone rang at that precise moment.

Trench Doll was calling him on FaceTime.

Trey's lips spread apart to reveal both rows of teeth — a criminal's smile. He glanced over at Thirty and answered the call.

"Where you at?" Trench Doll's voice came through loud and clear, the club music thumping hard in the background.

She was in the restroom; Trey could see the stalls behind her, one of which swung open as he spoke.

"In traffic," he said, watching as a BBW in a tight blue jumpsuit came walking out of the open stall behind her. "On my way there."

The corners of her mouth rose in a simpering smile. She thumbed her long weave from in front of her eye and tipped her head to the side.

"Boy, you done came a long way from rockin' them bogus ass True Religion jeans."

"You got me fucked up. On David, I ain't never rocked no—"

"Shut up. Dang. You can't tell when a bitch just playin' witchoo?" She puckered her rosy red lips and rolled her eyes. "I see dat li'l money you got."

"Ain't shit little about my money."

Trench Doll's eyes went up again. "You tryna fuck?" she asked, getting right to the point.

Trey's excited smile answered that question for him.

"Two hun'ed," Trench Doll said. "Gimme two hun'ed and we can do us."

"Bet. Bet that up"

"I should tax yo' ass," she said, her eyes wide and playful.

"Fuck outta here." Trey adjusted his arm in its powder blue sling. "I'll be there in about fifteen minutes. Have one of dem bottles on ice for me. We goin' straight up to the Champagne Rooms wit' gang n'em. You can bring yo' li'l buddies up there, too."

"I got everything you need right here," she said, her smile not quite reaching her eyes. She panned the camera quickly, showing her red, skintight dress. It was a Chanel number, with a long slit up the right thigh. "Don't make me wait."

Thirty was already shaking his head as Trey ended the call and slipped the phone into his sling.

"Dumbass," Thirty said.

"That bitch wouldn't dare play wit' me. You know it like I know it. Especially not over Lamron Dre. That nigga ain't never gave her a dollar."

"I don't know why you think you so fuckin' invincible," Thirty snapped. "That's the grimiest bitch ever came outta our projects. I think she the one set up Edai. She used to set niggas up for me and Dank all the time."

Shaking his head in frustration, Thirty leaned forward and tapped their driver on the shoulder. The man looked back.

"Change of plans," Thirty said. "This genius back here ain't thinkin' clearly."

"Let his dick think for him?" The driver laughed. "I know the struggle. Just tell me where y'all need me to go and I gotchoo."

Trey's expression hardened. He turned to glower at his big brother, balling his right hand in a fist and liking the subtle pain that resonated from the bullet hole in his shoulder. That ache reminded him of how his girlfriend had betrayed him over a Facebook crush, and how that Facebook crush of hers was the reason why Rello, one of his closest childhood friends, was now nothing more than a cold slab of meat and bone on a coroner's table.

"Nahhh, nigga," he said, shifting his attention back to the driver. "We ain't duckin' shit. We gettin' dropped off right in front of the club. I wish that bitch would try to set me up. Her whole family gon' die. On Big A grave, I'll kill dat bop-ass ho right then and there."

"Trey, look at me," Thirty said, his voice dropping an octave. "If we pull up out there and I see one thing outta place — one car full'a niggas just sittin' there, one nigga standin' where he shouldn't be — we ain't stoppin'. I don't care about no Trench Doll, and I definitely don't give a fuck about your ego. You hear me?"

Trey didn't answer. He was too busy looking at his own "live" feed, watching the fire emojis stack up, completely deaf to the sound of the trap door swinging shut.

Chapter 29

Vielle and her three friends ended up spending a lot more than a couple of minutes inside her bullet-riddled house.

For three hours they cleaned and cleaned, sweeping up the wood shavings from the doors that hadbeen replaced, and the glass from the windows that had been shot out, and the dried splotches of blood from Tom-Tom, Flower, and Journee.

Vielle's hands were raw from the bleach. She kept scrubbing at a dark, stubborn mahogany stain near the baseboard where Journee had stood playing and eating a drumstick just twenty-four hours ago.

"Vee, stop," Bambi said, touching her shoulder. "You gon' be done peeled the finish off the wood."

Vielle didn't stop scrubbing. She couldn't . If she could just get the floor clean, maybe the house wouldn't feel like a tomb. Beside her, the heavy frame of the Glock 21 sat on a stack of clean towels, a silent reminder that she was no longer just a victim.

"He's live," Tonya whispered from the couch, her eyes glued to her phone screen. "Trey. He's in the backseat of somebody's truck with Thirty, stuntin' with a bunch'a money on his lap, like he didn't just kill a whole baby. Look at this nigga." She turned the phone so they could see Trey for themselves. "See? He act like he ain't got a care in the world."

Vielle stopped scrubbing then. She looked at the phone, then at her new gun, her eyes turning as cold as the wind over Lake Michigan.

"His ass is dead, y'all. I swear on the life he took, I don't care how I gotta do it, he ain't gon' live too much longer. If Lorde don't get him somebody else will."

Her words were so heavy that none of her friends wanted to pick them up. Everyone just stared at her, their mouths shut, their eyes wide as silver dollars.

Vielle was rising from her knees when the low, aggressive rumble of a HEMI engine vibrated through the floorboards. She didn't me to look out the window to know the sound — that was Meko's jet black Dodge Charger SRT.

She stood up, wiping her bleach-laden hands on her jeans, and picked up her Glock. She stepped out onto the porch just as the Charger's doors swung open.

There were two more cars behind the Charger — a dull green 1980's-model Chevy Caprice Classic on huge gold-spoked rims and a silver, newer model Cadillac CT5. Both cars were filled with members of BG's Money Gang clique, and they hopped out seconds after BG and Meko did.

Meko stepped out of the driver's door of the Charger, looking like the fearless young man he was. He was holding an all-white AR-15 down by his side, the stark ceramic finish of the rifle gleaming under the streetlights. Baby Gang climbed out from the passenger side, gripping a Mini Draco with a high-capacity drum magazine that made it look heavy and lethal.

Baby Gang jogged up the porch steps, his eyes softening when they landed on Vee. He wrapped his long arms around her and hugged, glancing left and right to keep an eye on 7th Street as he did it.

"Just the person I needed to see," he said, looking down at her with the world's most handsome smile stretched across his lips. "I ain't tryna get you drawn into this shit or nothin' like that, but I'ma need you to tell me where dude stay at. I know it's somewhere in Southgate, but I need the address."

"224 Pine Tree Court, apartment 102," Vee replied without a second's hesitation. "And when you find him, kill him. Please. I ain't got much in the bank but—"

"Stop it. If anything we'll pay you," Baby Gang said, turning to stand beside her, his gaze flicking up and down the block. "That address was all I came to get... Well, that and..."

He trailed off, looking over at her with a certain kind of look on his face. Vielle couldn't quite decipher the meaning to that look, but she knew deep down in her soul that she liked it. He seemed so tall standing next to her, and he smelled so incredibly good. He wore a fresh brown leather Pelle Pelle jacket over tan-colored, loose-fitting cargo pants and wheat-colored Timberland boots, as if he'd gone all in on trying to match up his fit with the laminated birch wood handguard at the front end of his Draco.

"That and what?" Vee asked, tucking her gun in the back of her jeans — since she clearly no longer needed it. "Don't leave me hangin'. Speak your mind."

She couldn't stop looking at him from the corner of her eye. She liked the rich dark smoothness of his skin complexion, and how nonchalantly he seemed to go about his days. She liked the wisdom conveyed in his social media posts — he was forever posting about the importance of remaining loyal to friends and family, uplifting the community, and being a genuinely good human.

He was also very good in bed; she liked that attribute especially.

He was opening his mouth to speak when an older model Buick turned the corner from Willard Avenue on to 7th Street. It was a rusted, champagne-colored LeSabre, and Vee had never seen it ride past her house before.

She reached behind her back and drew her pistol. Baby Gang raised his, as did Meko. The doors on the CT5 and the heavy Chevy flew open, and Money Gang hopped out seven-deep, all eyes on the slow-moving Buick.

The car moved with a predatory slowness, it's suspension sagging low over the rear tires. The faces it's passengers were barely discernible in the darkness of the windshield, and the tint on the side windows was bubbling and dark, making it impossible to see who was behind the wheel. The harsh, grating thump-thump-thump of the Buick's blown muffler echoed off the narrow houses.

"Hold on," Baby Gang muttered, his thumb sliding toward the safety of his Draco.

Meko didn't say a word. He simply leveled his AR-15 at the street, accidentally stepping down onto one of the teddy bears that had been left at the foot of the porch steps as he moved back a couple of feet.

In the doorway behind Vee, Tonya let out a muffled gasp, her hand flying to her mouth as the Buick drifted to the curb two houses down. The rest of Money Gang started cracking their doors, the metallic snick of chambering rounds punctuating the silence.

Ancient brake pads made a small screech as the Buick came to a halt. For three infinite seconds everyone held their breaths. Then, the driver's door groaned open with a loud, rusty creak.

An elderly woman, no taller than five feet and wearing a floral Sunday hat that had seen better times, shuffled out. She squinted through thick eyeglasses, oblivious to the small army of high-caliber weapons aimed at her chest. She reached into the backseat and pulled out a fat leather purse.

"Excuse me, young man!" she chirped, waving an arthritic hand at Meko. "Do you know where I can find New Hope Missionary Baptist Church? I was told it was right here somewhere, but all I see is houses."

The tension snapped like the old lady's hip might if she fell the wrong way. Baby Gang sighed and lowered his

Draco, Meko laughed, and Vee pointed toward the opposite end of the block.

"It's down there, ma'am. On the left. Right at the corner of 7th and Lamb."

In the doorway behind Vee, Tonya, Bambi, and Kela exploded into frantic, nervous laughter, the adrenaline drop making their knees weak.

"Y'all , come on in before we fuck around and air out somebody's grandmama," Vee said.

She led the way in and stood by the door until the last member of Money Gang was inside. Then she locked the door and led them through the house to the basement door, which stood in the kitchen near the back door.

"I got everything down here," she said, opening the door. "A bed, two leather couches and some chairs I got from Rent-A-Center, a TV with a PS5 — the whole enchilada."

Baby Gang's boys went jetting down the rickety wooden steps as soon as Vee mentioned the PS5. She laughed and shook her head.

"You ain't gon' be able to get these niggas to leave," Baby Gang said as Vee's girlfriends slipped around them to follow the boys downstairs. "Especially if you got some Call of Duty or NBA 2K26."

"Check and check."

Victor Lewis chuckled. Vielle Gaing simpered, scissoring her thick legs and looking down at the pink toe-ends of her Air Jordan 1 Retro High OG "Atmosphere" sneakers. The navy blue on her shoes anchored the blue of her jeans, and her ballet slipper-pink Loro Piana sweater was a cashmere turtleneck. Her jewelry consisted of a small pair of hoop earrings and a thin gold necklace with a grooved gold cross for a pendant. She smelled like bleach, but she knew that she was looking as good as ever.

Baby Gang couldn't stop staring at her.

"You were saying?" she said, still eyeing her shoes. "On the porch, I mean. You started to tell me something, but then that lady pulled up."

"I know." He breathed in and breathed out. Set his Draco on the kitchen counter and pushed his fingertip through a bullet hole in the doorframe. "Damn, I'm bad at this kinda shit."

"Bad at what?" Vielle thought she knew what kinda shit he was talking about, and she was anxious to hear him say it.

"Look." He sighed. "Last night, that threesome…"

"What about it?"

"I know it might be, might be kinda…kinda hard to even think about fuckin' wit' a nigga who fucked yo' friend, but shit, I want you to rock wit' me. On some relationship type shit. I mean, if that's coo—"

"Yes!" Vee brought her hand up to cover her mouth, embarrassed at how eager she'd sounded. "I mean, yes. Yes. I like you, too. And I'm single, so…" She hitched her shoulders. "I'm down."

Her words gave Baby Gang all the courage he needed. He put his hands on her hips and pulled her closer, the cold leather of his Pelle Pelle jacket pressing against the soft, expensive warmth of her cashmere sweater. When she looked up, he didn't hesitate. He leaned down and kissed her, his mouth tasting like the mint of a Newport. It wasn't a hesitant "first-date" kiss; it was heavy and masculine, the kind of kiss that melts a woman down like an overused candle.

Vielle let her eyes flutter shut, her hands finding the rough texture of his jacket. For a second or two, the strong scent of bleach on her skin was replaced by his expensive cologne. The basement door was thin, and the muffled sounds of NBA 2K26 and the girls' laughter vibrated through the floorboards, but in the kitchen, the air was still. It was a promise made in a house that felt like a funeral home — a spark of something new right there where so much had been lost.

Chapter 30

"Mark My Words," another of Rap Lorde's more popular songs, played at a low volume inside Lorde's clean gray Trackhawk.

That was the only sound to be heard.

Sipping Lean from his doubled-up Styrofoam cups and staring straight ahead at the strip club across the street, Lorde was in the daze of memories.

He remembered Journee's first steps. She was just eight months old when that milestone moment happened. He and Crystal were in Paris, France at the time, staying at the Hôtel de Crillon on the Place de la Concorde, in the $25,000-a-night Bernstein Suite.

Designed by the late Karl Lagerfeld, the Bernstein was a 2,500-square-foot residence, the kind of place where the butler knew your daughter's favorite stuffed animal and kept the fridge stocked with her preferred brand of milk. Journee's first four steps were taken in a room with silver-flecked marble floors softened by hand-woven silk rugs that felt like clouds underfoot — the perfect, plush landing spot for Journee's first tumble.

Then there was the time she'd met her favorite cartoon character, Bluey. Hard's fifty-year-old brother, James Gaing Jr, was Lorde's road manager at that time, handling everything for the West Coast leg of the "Lorde of the Streets" tour — a run that had seen Lorde clear nearly a million dollars win profit after the smoke cleared. Instead of a penthouse suite, they'd taken over the Royal Oak Estate in

Encino, California, a sprawling hilltop rental made of glass, steel, and white stone. Lorde remembered the driveway being clogged with blacked out SUVs and a security detail of dark-suited armed with enough weaponry to end a war.

Inside, the house was a museum of cold marble and vaulted ceilings, but June 19th of 2025, Journee's fifth birthday, the back wing had been transformed into a five-year-old's kingdom.

Lorde remembered how the heavy glass doors had open to the patio. Journee had been mid-sprint, her little brown feet thumping against the polished stone, when she skidded to a halt. Standing right there on the opposite side of the open patio door, framed by the neon-blue glow of the infinity pool and the sparkling lights of the San Fernando Valley below, were life-sized versions of Bluey and Bingo.

The reaction was much more than a smile; it was a squealing system override. Journee's jaw dropped, her eyes went wide as saucers, and then she let out a high-pitched, ear-piercing shriek that echoed off the glass walls. She'd practically launched herself at them, her tiny hands reaching out to grab Bluey's plush blue fur.

Lorde had stood back, his jewelry catching the fading California sun, watching his daughter go practically insane with joy. For those few hours, there were no contracts, no rivalries, no tour dates. There was just a father watching his daughter play "Keepy Uppy" with a giant cartoon dog in a mansion that cost more than the neighborhood he grew up in.

Now, sitting in the Trackhawk with tears flowing freely from his red-veined eyes, Lorde trembled with rage at the idea of that joyous shriek being permanently silenced. The condensation on his cup felt like ice against his hand. The memory of that high-pitched laughter felt a million miles away from the neon lights of the strip club and the heavy silence of the dark parking lot across the street. He took another slow sip, the "Mark My Words" beat playing like a distant heartbeat in the background. The ghost of Journee's joy faded back into the dark recesses of his brain, and he put his cup in his cup holder to hold his gun in both hands.

The Micro Draco resting on Lorde's lap was a vicious, compact piece of machinery — the shortest version of the Romanian-designed pistol, stripped down to a barrel just over six inches long. The original wood handguard had been swapped out for an aftermarket black rail with a tactical flashlight taped to the side. A heavy, translucent 40-round polymer magazine curved out from the magwell, loaded with 7.62×39mm rounds that could punch through car doors like paper. Without a stock, the heavy metal receiver ended in a simple sling swivel, making it awkward for most but deadly in close quarters for someone who knew how to handle the kick.

Lorde's fingers traced the steel receiver as he sat in the driver's of his Trackhawk, listening to Fayzo and Lil Luke as they talked to Trench Doll on the phone. She said Trey was on his way now, and she was coming out to get her money before the shit hit the fan.

Across the street, the heavy front doors of the strip club swung open. Trench Doll stepped out onto the neon glow, scanning the block before locking eyes with Lorde through the windshield of his Trackhawk. She smoothed down her dress and stepped off the curb, intending to cross the street to pick up her five grand for the "lo" she'd dropped on Trey and his brother Thirty.

She only made it three steps before a pair of incoming headlights blinded her.

An orange Santa Fe came barreling down Lake Street, its engine roaring as it tore past. The Uber driver, whose nerves were already shot from listening to Thirty's concerns over possibly being set up, slammed his foot down on the brake to keep fromhitting Trench Doll. The tires shrieked and burned against the asphalt, the SUV jerking violently as it slid to a halt.

In those chaotic seconds of braking, the Uber driver's eyes darted around the street. He noticed the two dark Trackhawks parked directly across from the club two seconds before Thirty did.

In the backseat of the Santa Fe, Thirty's eyes finally clocked the Trackhawks, but by then it was already too late.

Across the street in the JKS Ventures parking lot , Lorde's gaze locked onto the front windshield of the idling SUV. He spotted Thirty's face under the glow of the streetlights.

"That't them! That's them niggas right there!" Lorde yelled, his voice jarring his two younger passengers to action.

In a synchronized blitz, Lorde, Fayzo, Lil Luke, and Terry Lee reached up and yanked their black Shiesty masks down over their faces, leaving only their eyes exposed. Their doors flew open, and they bailed out of the two Trackhawks on foot, hitting the pavement with their weapons raised. The four of them aimed straight at the Santa Fe, opening fire before their feet even cleared the gravel.

There was no time to hesitate when even the most fleeting instance of hesitation could mean certain death. Thirty kicked his door open, aiming a Glock 23 over the frame. The gun was fitted with a huge and heavy 50-round drum magazine, and attached to the back of the slide was a small, silver "switch" — the illegal conversion modification that turned the semi-automatic pistol into a fully automatic machine gun. Thirty pulled the, and the Glock screamed, unleashing a torrent of .40-caliber rounds in a single, deafening spray.

The Santa Fe was still screeching to a stop when Trey threw open his door and jumped out of the rear passenger side. He pointed his .45 and opened fire, holding the heavy gun straight out and shooting with one hand, his arm absorbing the sharp recoil as he tracked the incoming shooters.

Terry Lee was in the lead on Lorde's side, sprinting the fastest, his own modified Glock rattling as he held back the trigger. Both Trey and Thirty focused their fire on him.

Terry squeezed off a stream of gunfire from his Glock, and one of the rounds tore right through the middle part of Trey's left thigh — one quick, through-and-through wounds that painted Trey's Burberry-checked pants red. But Trey didn't let up. He and Trey kept firing, their rounds chewing up Terry Lee's chest. One of Thirty's .40-caliber bullets caught Terry Lee square in the throat, snapping his head back like a running dog at the end of his leash.

That throat shot took all the momentum from Terry Lee's legs, and he crashed hard into the street. He rolled onto his back, clutching weakly at his neck, choking on his own blood as life drained from him beneath the flashing neon lights.

But the numbers were entirely on Lorde's side. Lorde stepped up, raising the Micro Draco just above his waist, and fired a rapid succession of 7.62-millimeter rounds directly into Thirty chest and gut. At the same time, Fayzo and Lil Luke rushed up with their AR pistols, unleashing a hailstorm of high-velocity gunfire into Thirty's chest and face. Dozens more rounds stitched across Thirty's torso and limbs. Put up against that kind of coordinated firepower, Thirty didn't stand a chance; his brains blew west and his body went south, crumpling beside the open rear door of the Santa Fe, his gun falling silent next to him.

Through the haze of gunsmoke, Trey saw Trench Doll screaming, turning on her heel to run back toward the safety of the strip club. This bitch set me up, Trey thought, seeing the setup clear as day. He pivoted his .45 and three quick rounds into her back — PHOW PHOW PHOW! The bullets dropped her right outside The Gold Room's front door, mortally wounded and gasping on the concrete.

Shifting his attention back to the surviving gangsters, he let off five more blind shots and ended up catching Fayzo directly in the stomach. Fayzo doubled over with a guttural groan, dropping his AR pistol and clutching the fat round holes in his midsection as he hit the pavement, severely wounded but still breathing.

Now caught in a desperate, one-armed shootout against three heavily armed opps, Trey knew his time had run out. His thigh was burning, and his ammunition was low. As a civilian sedan slowed down to avoid the gunfire, Trey lunged toward the driver's side, ripped the terrified female motorist out of the front seat, and threw himself behind the wheel. It didn't even register in his mind that he had carjacked a 2026 Bentley Flying Spur Mulliner from the daughter of an Italian mob boss, and he never would have imagined that the body of a crooked federal prosecutor might lay dead and hog-tied in the trunk. He was merely looking for an escape from certain death, and so he made his daring escape, fishtailing off down Lake Street as the masked shooters ventilated the Bentley's trunk area with their mini assault rifles.

For Lil Luke and Lorde, the scene they were left with was chaos. Still spraying rounds at Trey as he raced way, they rushed over to Fayzo's groaning body and began carrying him by his jacket and arms, dragging his boots across the asphalt before hoisting him up between them. They moved hurriedly back toward the open doors of Lorde's smoke-gray Trackhawk, leaving the bloody casualties of the shootout for a Stone Park coroner to sort out.

Chapter 31

Trey gripped the leather-wrapped steering wheel of the Bentley in a tight-knuckled fist, his left leg twitching involuntarily as blood from his shot-through thigh pooled onto the deep-pile lamb's wool floor mat. The twin-turbocharged engine of the Flying Spur roared, a deep, bottomless purr that felt completely detached from the hell he'd just left behind on Lake Street. His left shoulder was numb and trembling from adrenaline and all that bone-shaking recoil, his ears ringing so loud he could hardly hear the wind whistling through the bullet holes stitched across the rear glass — well, not so much bullet holes as they were markings, as if the bullets had flattened on impact instead of passing through the glass.

He didn't know who owned this luxurious car, and honestly he didn't care; it was fast, it was armored enough to take a shower of high-caliber rifle rounds to the trunk, and it was getting him away from a Micro Draco and two AR pistols.

"Keep it together, keep it together," he growled through gritted teeth, glancing down at his Burberry pants. They were ruined, soaked completely through in an ever-widening crimson. The through-and-through hole in his thigh burned like promiscuous pussy. He needed to find a dark, isolated spot where he could pull over and tie off his leg before he fainted from blood loss behind the wheel of some stranger's four-hundred-thousand-dollar car.

Pulling off the main strip into a deserted alley near the border of Melrose Park, Trey slammed the Bentley into park. The cabin fell into a high-tech, suffocating silence, save for the hum of the climate control. He threw open the driver's door and limped clumsily to the back of the blacked-out Flying Spur to check the damage, again gripping his Glock .45 in his hand.

The rear of the Mulliner edition was peppered with jagged entry holes from two ARPs and a Micro Draco. Trey reached down and hit the electronic trunk release, intending to check and see if the gas tank had been struck by gunfire, and if he could find a First Aid kit.

The trunk lid whined and lifted automatically, casting a soft LED light over the cargo space — a space that, miraculously, hadn't been penetrated by any of the rounds.

Trey's breath caught in his throat. His hand froze on his gun. His phone rang in his pocket, a ring that could have originated in Pakistan, it sounded so far away.

There was no luggage. No First Aid kit. Instead, cramped into the luxurious, carpeted trunk space, was the stiff body of a middle-age white man in a rumpled blue suit. He was hog-tied with heavy-duty zip ties, a thick strip of silver duct tape slapped across his mouth, his wide, lifeless eyes staring straight up at the sky. Trey instantly recognized the face from the local news stations — it was Patrick Vance, the high-profile federal prosecutor who had been missing for the last forty-eight hours.

Trey stared at the corpse, his own bleeding leg suddenly forgotten as a cold sweat broke out across his neck. He looked around the desolate alley, searching for cameras, faces in windows — anyone who could point him out in a lineup.

Whose Bentley had he taken?

Chapter 32

Inside Lorde's stormcloud-gray Trackhawk, the air no longer smelled like expensive cologne and sweet Lean. It smelled like blood, burnt gunpowder, and panic.

Lorde threw the high-performance SUV into reverse to back up in a smoking roar of tires, then he shot forward out of the parking lot at a wild, reckless speed. Stomping his foot down on the gas pedal, he launched the vehicle down the dark asphalt of Lake Street, the hazard lights flashing from the sudden acceleration.

In the backseat, Lil Luke was sweating through his Shiesty mask, his hands trembling as he applied desperate pressure to the fat, leaking holes in Fayzo's stomach. Fayzo's blood was already soaking into the pristine gray leather seats, turning the luxury interior into a slaughterhouse.

"He bleedin' out, big bro!" Lil Luke shouted, his eyes wide with panic. "He ain't talkin'!" Fayzo was unconscious, his chest rising in shallow, ragged hitches, a pink foam bubbling at the corners of his mouth.

Lorde's eyes looked bloodshot and wild in the rearview mirror, tears of rage and grief tracking through the dryness of his face. He checked the street behind him. Terry Lee's body was a dark shape fading into the distance in the street outside The Gold Room, Thirty's head and torso resembled a butchered tomato, and Trench Doll lay dead by the entrance. They had caught one of their targets, but looking at Terry Lee way back there in the street and his fellow gang member fading out in the backseat, the victory felt hollow.

"Keep pressure on them bullet wounds!" Lorde's voice boomed over the roar of the engine. Don't let him close his eyes, Luke! Keep him woke!"

Lorde tore through a red light, swerving around a delivery truck — and nearly sideswiping it —as he raced toward the city. They couldn't go to a regular ER — not with the weapons they'd just used in a brutal murder, a wounded man in the backseat, and a trail of bodies in left in Stone Park. He needed to get to Dr. Jackson, the dirty, cash-hungry surgeon in Maywood who took his blue faces up front and kept his mouth shut for the cartels, undocumented immigrants, and hood rich street niggas like Lorde.

He gripped the steering so hard two of his knuckles popped, his mind racing as fast as the Trackhawk's speedometer. They had ended Thirty, but the man who shot Fayzo — the man who'd just disappeared in a shot-to-hell Bentley — was still breathing.

Lorde wasn't going to stop until the Chicago pavement ran red with his blood, too.

Chapter 33

Three Days Later

Hard awoke to the soulful crooning of Tazera Williams humming along to Kehlani's "Folded" while she literally refolded the clothes she'd just taken out of cardboard box marked Candy's Top Drawers.

The music was playing from her daughter Tayda's iPhone, as Tayda stood nervous in the bedroom doorway, watching Hard sit up and yawn and thumb the crust from the corners of his eyes.

It was hard to believe that only three days had passed since he was released from prison. In those three days he'd gone from being flat broke after having to pay cash for a house to having made over a hundred grand off the cocaine he'd gotten from Tone Bone. He'd blown $35,000 at Dan's Furniture to furnis his new home, and Dan hadn't disappointed. There was rich brown leather in the living room and sitting room, and Barclay Butera Malibu bedroom sets in all five of the bedrooms.

"Why you standin' way over there?" Hard asked, cracking his first grin of the day. "You was all eager to meet me when I was in the joint. Now a nigga home and you wanna act all shy."

"Whatever." Tayda's face lit up, but she remained timid, slowly stepping deeper into the room. "I just don't like violating people's personal space. Because whenever I stay the night over here, I don't want nobody just walking in on me."

"Girl, please," Candy said, glancing back over her shoulder. "I'm walkin' right in there. I don't care if you got that bum you call a boyfriend in there with you or not."

"See, you ain't finna be talkin' about my man " Tayda laughed. She was slim and pretty, several shades darker than her mother, but they had the same face, the same smile, the same walk. Even their laughs were similar.

Hard swung his legs over the side of the bed and yawned. His phones were on the nightstandboth of them fully charged. He took them into the bathroom with him and didn't even turn them on. He liked his peace in the morning, especially before he had his coffee.

In the shower he ruminated over his week so far. He'd already made $215,000 off the fifty-five bricks of coke, selling thirty-five of them to a rich young dope boy named Kirk B in Dayton, Ohio, and having the younger members of his organization deal the rest. With the aid of some guys who were still behind the wall and a few who were in the free world with him, he'd established a team of loyal soldiers — gang members from just about every branch of the Almighty Vice Lord Nation — to sell his drugs and hold his security whenever he needed to go out in public. He had a trap house on the west side, a trap house on the east side, and an entire neighborhood to push the coke through in Chicago.

Vielle's new boyfriend was one of the boys who'd fallen in under Hard's leadership. As soon as he learned of Hard's rank in the mob he and the Vice Lords in his Money Gang clique met up with Keezy and Shamar, who'd given them several of the Glocks and Hellpups from Hard's crates and put them in position.

Hard dried off and returned to the bedroom with only a towel wrapped around him. Candy rushed her teenage daughter out of the room: "Go, go, go, go, go," she said, pushing and shoving a laughing Tayda out of the room and slamming the door behind her.

Hard turned on his phones and checked his messages while Candy lotioned him down.

"We need to be heading straight out if you want to make that lunch on time. That Friday traffic gon' be hell in the next hour or so."

Hard nodded his agreement, staring wantonly at the tight gray leather pants Candy had on, and the snug-fitting gray-and-white Fendi sweater that perfectly outline her perfect C-cup boobs, and the brick-red Fenty lipstick that made her already juicy lips appear even juicier. Her hair was done up in a razor-sharp, asymmetrical bob that had cost Hard $1,500 for the hair alone. Her fingernails were long and stiletto-tipped, with an intricate pattern of Swarovski clustered at the base of her cuticles. She'd spent all afternoon yesterday getting her hair and nails done for today's lunch in Chicago.

Hard didn't see what the big deal was. He knew that Pastor Gregory Newsome, the pastor from his mother's old church, had organized the event, and that Tone Bone had helped out with the guest list, which pretty much guaranteed a roomful of old friends and former associates. He even knew that Serita, his old flame, was supposed to be there. But he still didn't see why everyone was so worked up over the event. He'd already had one "welcome home" party; he didn't need another one.

But there was no way he was going to turn down going to the party. For one, it was being held at RPM Steak, arguably the most exclusive steakhouse in all of Chicago. For two, if not for Tone Bone, he wouldn't be anywhere near as financially comfortable as he was now. And for three, Pastor Newsome was a good man with connections. He led one of the largest congregations in the Chicagoland area, a huge megachurch in Tinley Park that seated eight thousand. This powerful position gave Pastor Newsome massive political and social sway over suburban families and city politicians, and that was the kind of ally Hard needed if he planned on staying out of prison while simultaneously leading a rapidly growing circle of gang-affiliated drug dealers.

"How'd you meet that famous pastor?" Candy asked, her hands moving in circular motions as she rubbed the Palmer's cocoa butter lotion into his broad, muscular chest. "I remember seeing him on TV a lot around the time all those Black Lives Matter marches first started. I watch him on TV some Sundays when I come up to see my grandma in Chicago. She loves that man."

"I've known him since I was a kid." Hard's gaze grew vacant as the memories came back to him. "He, uhh…he wasn't always a man of God. I'll leave it at that."

Greg had, in fact, been assigned the role of Chief Enforcer for the Dark Side TVLs way back in the early nineties, when Hard was just a teenager running the streets of the Lawndale neighborhood with the rest of the gang. Hard and Tone Bone had witnessed Greg gun down a man called Stank in front of a gambling house near the corner of 16th and Millard Avenue. The man had owed the TVLs a few thousand dollars over some missing drugs, and when James — Chief of the Dark Side TVLs at that time — got tired of waiting, he'd sent a hit squad to delete the problem altogether.

Hard could remember it like it was yesterday. Him and Tone Bone keeping watch on Stank's Millard Avenue home from the alley behind Dvorak High School until he returned home from work. Then, when Stank's midnight blue 1988 Oldsmobile Cutlass Supreme Classic rounded the corner, Hard signaled for Greg, who was lying down behind a row of bushes next to Stank's house.

Tone Bone, eager to witness his first murder, had walked further down the alley for a better view, and as soon as Stank parked that clean-ass Cutlass Greg had stood up and ran right to him, holding a sawed-off 12-gauge shotgun straight out in front of him. There was a stentorian BOOM! and a huge spray of blood and brain splashed across the inner windshield.

"Daaaaaaamn," Tone Bone had murmured, and Hard was surprised to hear himself repeating that same elongated word now, making Candy look up at him with her brow knitted in confusion.

"What? Why'd you just say that?" she asked.

Hard mouth smiled, but apparently that expression didn't reach his eyes, because Candy squinted at him and stuck out her bottom lip.

Hard kissed that jutting lip. He would have sucked on it had she not shoved him back following the initial peck.

"You are not about to mess up my makeup, nor am I about to let you mess up my hair. Wait until after the lunch."

"What if I want you for lunch?"

Candy rolled her eyes and turned away from him. "That's gon' have to wait, too. At least until after we get there. Maybe we can sneak off somewhere."

Hard took hold of Candy's wrist and snatched her back to him. He picked her up by the waist, letting his towel crumple to the floor and leaving him stark naked in the middle of their bedroom floor.

"What if I don't wanna wait?" He kissed the left side of her neck, then the right side, then the hollow spot at the base of her throat, all while holding her in the air as her legs ran an imaginary race.

"Boy, let me go!" she laughed, smacking him on the top of his bald head.

Hard flared his nostrils and inhaled the heavenly scent of her perfume. It was the $500 bottle of Amouage Guidance 46 he'd bought her a couple of months ago. He was always doing things like that, buying her clothes and shoes and perfume, roses and edible arrangements and sex toys, anything to spice things up and make her happy. He loved Candy, from the top of her head to the bottom of her feet, and he never let her forget it.

The urge to have her right now was almost too overwhelming to bear, but she was right. They needed to get going if they wanted to make it to the restaurant at a reasonable time.

"Hope I don't fuck around and get pulled over," Hard said, lowering Candy to the floor. "You know I ain't supposed to be leaving the county. I could violate parole if—"

"Nope." Candy pressed a silencing forefinger to his lips. "I already called and got permission from your P.O. He says he knows your pastor from TV, and to text him when we make it back home later today." She turned to leave, snapping her fingers twice as she said, "Now hurry up, snap-snap. We ain't got all day."

Chapter 34

Trey was in an ocean of grief over the loss of his brother. He'd been in bed ever since he left the hospital three nights ago. His crutches were leaned against the wall next to the nightstand, where his prescription pill bottles stood like white-hatted soldiers.

Both of the bullets that hit his thigh had done extensive damage, but his dead father's military background and VA connections had gotten him the best treatment money could buy. Even so, the damage was bad, and there would be a long road to recovery.

He was at Thirty's place in Chicago Heights, in an east wing bedroom that was far away from the renovations currently underway on the west wing. All the hammering and drilling was keeping him up, but the opioids had him too high to care — and besides, his brother was dead. Bryshon Perry, alias Thirty, was as dead as King Von, Odee, Big A, and all the rest of O Block's fallen soldiers. All the guys were making social media posts about Thirty's murder, promising "get back" for his death. All of Trey's cousins and uncles were ready to go to war with the Dark Side TVLs and whoever their allies were. His cousin Boy Boy had already slid through 16th Street and opened fire on a crowd of people who probably had nothing to do with Thirty's death.

But what good did any of that do when no one knew where to find Lorde? He was practically rich, his drug money and rap checks allowing him the freedom to go wherever he wanted to go. He could buy all the guns and ammunition he needed for the war, and he could hide out in the meantime, sending the younger, poorer members of his gang on murder missions and paying them when they scored. If Trey was going to catch up with Lorde, he'd have to find someone close to the drill rapper and get them to flip — and that would take time.

During the few instances when the pain meds didn't have Trey all the way out of it, he'd contemplated the idea of sending his fellow gang members to shoot up Journee Gaing's funeral. The only thing was, no one knew where that funeral was going to take place. On top of that, Journee's uncle HJ was a homicide detective, so there would likely be a heavy police presence at that funeral. You couldn't just come through and shoot up that kind of event, not without expecting your own funeral in the very near future.

And then there was the issue of the dead federal prosecutor in the trunk of that blacked-out, shot-to-hell Bentley Flying Spur.

He'd ditched the car in an empty garage next to an abandoned house on the east side of Chicago Heights, in a section of the neighborhood just a couple of blocks away from the notoriously treacherous Wentworth Apartments.

"Trey, you good in here? Need something to drink or eat?"

It was Tadda Mae, Thirty's ex-girlfriend and the mother of his son and daughter.

She pushed open the door and peeked her head in, a gorgeous round visage framed by an expensive lace front wig the color of freshly picked lemons. Her skin complexion was strawberry-brown, and her eyelashes were far too long to be real. She watched him through the reflection of the dresser mirror across the room from him.

"Hell naw, I ain't nowhere near good. Bitch-ass niggas killed my brudda. I'ma make it, though. Them niggas gon' pay in the end. On Lil Steve grave, this shit far from over."

Tadda Mae stepped inside. She was a short woman, five-five at the most, and she was as thick as thick could get, all surgically-fattened ass and thighs and titties. She'd left Thirty for a college football quarterback who'd recently gone pro, signing with the Seahawks for a reported $34.7 million. She'd gotten him to buy her a Ferrari SUV — a powder blue Purosangue worth more than $500,000 — and the million-dollar house she owned in Olympia Fields, and then he'd dumped her when photos surfaced of her in a hotel suite with an up-and-coming Chicago R&B singer.

Her hair nearly reached the floor. The yellow leather Hermès Birkin bag strapped to her shoulder was likely just as pricey as the Richard Mille watch she had strapped to her wrist, and the watch band was the same shade of yellow. She wore dark green pants with yellow camo designs and a matching sweatshirt with the word Balenciaga printed across the chest. Her earrings were fat gold hoops, and she wore diamond rings on the middle and ring fingers of both hands.

Trey gathered the strength to sit up as Tadda Mae came in and stood beside the bed looking down at him.

"I don't know how to tell you this," Tadda Mae said quietly, "but they got your picture on the news. For killing that five-year-old and somebody else in Michigan City."

Trey might have been in a drug-induced stupor, but he was alert enough to understand what he was facing. A double murder in Indiana meant a definite life sentence, especially when one of the victims was a toddler.

He looked at Tadda Mae. Her unparalleled beauty left him speechless for a moment. Then he licked his lips, sighed, and said, "Shit."

"Yeah," Tadda Mae said, as if his one-word response was a clear and concise statement. She picked up the TV remote and flipped to the news channels. When she didn't find what she was looking for she found it on her iPhone. "See? Look at this."

It was on abc7 News: Englewood Man Wanted in NW Indiana Double Homicide.

Trey read the article. It named him and Big Block as the main suspects in December 9th's double slaying. A third, unnamed suspect had been shot and killed the same day in Stone Park, Illinois. There was no word of a possible connection between the two cases, but Trey knew the connection. The unnamed suspect was his dead brother, which could only mean one thing — Big Block had folded.

"Shit," Trey muttered again.

"You should be okay here. Those construction workers should be gone in the next couple of hours. They finished connecting the bathroom to the master bedroom, and I cancelled the rest of the renovations. No sense in going through with them when Thirty's…"

She couldn't get the rest of it out. Her lips began to tremble, so she bit down on the bottom one. Tears welled up in her light brown eyes. A bubble of gas formed right inside Trey's asshole, but right now seemed like the wrong time for a fart, so he held it in.

"I feel like it's my fault," Tadda Mae sobbed. "Y'all would've never even heard of Michigan City if it wasn't for me. That's the only reason he moved you out there. I met him when I was dancing at Redbone's and we ended up going back to my place in MC and spending the rest of the summer there. He liked it so much that he got you an apartment in Southgate."

"You can't blame yourself for that shit." Trey's voice sounded dry, scratchy. His tongue felt numb from the pain meds. "If it's anybody's fault it's Vielle's. That funky bitch. She shot me. If she would'a never shot me, Baby Lord and that lil girl would'a never got shot. It's simple as that. She started this whole bullshit. That was her brother and his lil guys who killed bro."

"How would you know that? I saw the footage. They had masks on."

"Look at the other nigga who died out there. That was Terry Lee, Baby Lord's brother. All them niggas in the same gang. Cup Gang, Baby T Blood Gang — they all Travelers. TVLs. And all them niggas gon' die. For Thirty, for Rello. On David."

Tadda Mae sniffled. "Just tell me what I need to do. I'll help," she said, sobbing. "Them bitch-ass niggas killed my baby daddy. They k-killed him."

She went running from the room after that. Trey felt her pain. His heart was aching, as well, aching just as bad as his shoulder and thigh.

He swallowed down a thirty-milligram Percocet tablet and chased it with the glass of water Tadda Mae had brought in to him earlier. Within minutes he was nodding, dreaming about the shooting that had claimed his brother's life, only in his dream he saved Thirty from that brutal death, shooting down the masked gunmen as they sprinted in from that dark parking lot across the street.

When he woke at noon the noise of the construction crew had ceased. An episode of FBI was playing on the 115-inch Samsung TV. Unable to stomach the sight of any sort of police activity, Trey switched on Netflix and began watching Wake Up Dead: A Knives Out Mystery, which had just premiered that morning.

He wasn't focused for long. His mind kept drifting back to Lorde, wondering where he lived, what he was doing, who he was with. He also thought of Hard, the Gaing family's legendary patriarch. Both Hard and Lorde would soon die, if Trey had it his way.

And he was grimly determined to have it his way.

He lifted his phone from the end table and began searching for information regarding Baby Lord or Journee's funeral arrangements. There was nothing yet — at least not anything he could find — and before he could get before he could get back to stalking Rap Lorde's Instagram page he heard the gentle thumping of feminine footsteps moving toward him in the hallway. That fart bubble was back, resting right up against the inside of his sphincter. He needed to sit on the toilet for the first time in three days.

"Tadda, I need you to help me out this bed," he said. "I gotta use the bathroom."

No answer from the hallway.

The footfalls grew closer. Trey recognized the rhythmic clicking of high heels on wooden floorboards.

The door swung slowly open, and in walked an incredibly beautiful woman who looked so familiar to Trey that he was momentarily stunned. She had the kind of sharp, symmetrical bone structure that belonged on a billboard over Michigan Avenue, but there was nothing fragile about her. She reminded Trey of one of those supermodels you always saw in the designer fragrance commercials around the holidays. She had warm, rich olive skin and a cascading mane of espresso-black curls that fell past her shoulders. Her eyes were almond-shaped and aglow with an effortless confidence, her curves filling out her tailored, emerald green Gucci pantsuit in a way that seemed intentional and, to Trey, completely distracting.

The five athletically-built men who followed her into the room wore expensive-looking business suits, and one of them was holding Tadda Mae in front of him with her arm bent behind her back and a silver pistol pressed up against her temple. Two of the men took aim at Trey before he could even think of slipping his .45 from under his pillow.

"We finally meet," the HBIC said, regarding Trey with a bright-eyed grin. She walked up to Trey and reached out to shake his head. "Alessia Carbone. You're Trey, right? Treykwan Murray. Yeah, it's you." She nodded. "Just the man I was looking for. I believe you have something that belongs to me. Something pale…and cold…and white."

Her smile came on in a flash, an expression that could have been dragged straight from the pages of a Stephen King novel.

Trey quickly realized where he'd seen the woman. He'd put his gun to her head and snatched her out of the Bentley in front of The Gold Room.

The Flying Spur that had turned out to be a rolling hearse.

"Let her go," Trey said, his anger rising as he watched twin tears go streaking down Tadda Mae's pretty brown face. "On David Barksdale, shorty, if y'all don't let her go right the fuck now—"

Alessia Carbone ripped the blanket and sheet right off the bed, her horror story smile vanishing in an instant. Trey was wearing a gray and black pair of Ethika boxer briefs with a matching pair of Glory Gang socks and the icy Audemars Piguet watch Thirty had told Tadda Mae to bring to The Gold Room the other night.

"Do you have any fucking idea who you're talking to?!" She paused, as if seriously awaiting an answer; then: "Never mind that. Where's the fucking body?"

Trey only stared at the fine young woman, suddenly realizing that he'd seen her twice before — once outside the strip club three days ago, and once on CNN, when several members of Chicago's infamous Carbone Family were indicted by the FBI shortly before the COVID-19 pandemic hit.

"What's so important about a dead body?" Trey really wanted to know.

"That wasn't just any dead body, you fucking idiot. That was Patrick Vance. He's the guy who —"

"Prosecuted that cartel boss. Yeah, I remember that shit."

"Not just any cartel boss," Alessia said, crossing the room to look around in the closet. "Vance prosecuted Alejandro Villarreal, AKA El Verdugo. It means "The Executioner" in Spanish. Verdugo was in charge of the Gulf Cartel's assassination wing, but he moved kilos, too. Sometimes up to two metric tons of cocaine per month. The cartel isn't happy about losing their top assassin. They wanted that tough-shit prosecutor knocked off, and nobody was willing to take on that bounty."

"Nobody but you, huh?"

"Exactly."

Trey groaned and moaned as he shifted in the bed, slowly moving his wounded leg over the bedside and sitting all the way up. Alessia told the man holding Tadda Mae to free her arm from his grasp, and he did, but he kept his gun on her.

Trey made a promise to himself that he would kill that particular mobster. One way or the other, sooner or later, that man would die from a bullet to the brain for the way he was treating the mother of Thirty's children.

Tadda Mae rushed over to Trey's side. "Just tell them," she pleaded. "Just tell them whatever they need to know so they can go."

Trey shook his head from left to right. He was no rookie. He knew exactly what would happen if he told them where to find Patrick Vance's cold, dead corpse.

"How in the fuck did y'all find me?" he asked Alessia, but his eyes were on the man who'd held Tadda Mae at gunpoint. He was a stout man in shiny brown leather shoes and a spiffy gray suit-and-tie. His thinning brown hair was stiff and slicked back, likely with some sort of hair gel. His left ear was missing a piece of cartilage at the top of the lobe. He was chewing gum and sneering at Trey and Tadda Mae.

Alessia produced a small black rectangular device from her pocket. It looked like an old-school tape recorder, only there was a screen on one side that showed a flashing red dot and a satellite image of from just abovethe neighborhood they were currently in.

The red dot was flashing right on top of Thirty's house.

"Shit," Trey muttered as his mistake registered in his mind. "The Bentley key fob, huh? Got a tracker in it."

"You aren't as dumb as I thought you were." Alessia pocketed the device and placed her hands on her narrow hips. "Now," she said, taking the silver pistol from her gum-chewing crony and leveling it at Tadda Mae's forehead, "either you show me where you dumped that body or your little girlfriend here gets her pasta blown all over that bed." She sneered. "What's it gonna be?"

"Neither." Trey looked around at the men Alessia had behind her. "Kill her and watch how fast my lips seal shut. You'll have to kill me, too, and then you'll never find the body. And I got a question: How in the fuck did you manage to put a tracking device inside the key but not in the car itself?"

"There was one in the car." Alessia lowered her minion's gun a couple of inches, then a few more, and finally she held it down by her side and, with a despondent sigh, shook her head and fluttered her eyelashes. "We believe the tracker we had in the car was damaged in the shooting. It was embedded in the trunk lid."

"Aw yeah, that muhfucka's done for then." Trey found himself chuckling. "Them was choppa shells, seven-six-twos and five-five-sixes. I was wondering how they didn't blow right through the car and kill me. That was an armored car, wasn't it?"

Alessia gave him a nod. "B6 ballistic armor, stops everything but a three-oh-eight.Those AK and AR rounds didn't stand a chance." She started to raise the gun again, then changed her mind and ordered her men out of the room.

"Let me talk to them alone," she said. "Because we can't leave here without that body."

The man Trey wanted to kill turned to Alessia, his eyes going asquint. "There are ways to get that info without bowing down to these grease monkeys," he said, in a harsh, gravelly voice. "This guy's arm is in a sling, and his leg is wrapped in bandages. A kid could torture this scrawny fuck."

"Go, Pete." Alessia pointed to the open bedroom door, and her men headed out.

"Yeah, what she said," Trey said, mocking his newfound nemesis.

Pete glowered at him, but he didn't say anything as he trailed the other clean-suited goons out of the room.

In a flash, Trey swept his hand under his pillow and grabbed his Glock. He aimed it right at Alessia Carbone's face.

She didn't even flinch.

"El Verdugo," she said, as she began to pace back and forth in front of the dresser. "You know, he was under the Costilla Cartel umbrella — most of the cartels are these days — and they're pretty much done fucking around with the federal government. After El Chapo was sentenced to life plus thirty, all the cartels under the Costilla umbrella vowed to never let that happen to their leadership. So you can imagine how they must have felt when word came down that Verdugo was given three life sentences plus eighty years. Something had to be done."

Tadda Mae fell against Trey's bare shoulder, her canary-yellow waterfall of hair falling down over her face as she cried. Trey wanted to hug her,but he only had one arm to use, and that one was busy holding his Glock.

"So what's the bounty?" he asked the pacing Italian woman. "I want in. I'm wanted for a double murder right now, and I'm tryna get low for awhile. I could use some extra cash."

Alessia stopped pacing and looked at Trey with big eyes, her teeth showing in a stunned expression that some might classify as a smile.

"You got a deal. Lead us to the body before the police can get to it, and I'll give you a hundred grand. Cash. You can't beat that."

Tadda Mae squeezed Trey's elbow, and he immediately understood the meaning behind that sudden squeeze.

"Three hundred thousand," he said, and now he lowered his gun, too. "I'm a BD. We do everything in threes."

Alessia tilted her head so far forward that her chin might have touched her chest. She squinted like Pete, her hand tightening around the silver pistol.

"Deal," she said, after a time.

It was Trey's turn to smile.

"So where's the body?"

"I'll take you to it after y'all leave my brother's house, and after I get my money. Have somebody — and I mean one person — bring me the money. Once I count it out, I'll tell you exactly where to find that car."

Pete stepped back in the room. Alessia sighed, scratched her eyebrow with the barrel end of the gun, and then, with another sigh, she walked over to Trey and reached out to shake his hand. Unwilling to put down his .45, he shook with the hand that was cradled by the sling.

Something inside of him said he'd just made a deal with the devil, but he didn't really give a fuck, because he was a demon himself.

And besides, he needed the cash — not to flee from authorities, but to finance the war against Lorde and his gang.

Chapter 35

The heavy glass doors of RPM Steak swung open, and the modern, amber-lit warmth of the River North hotspot washed over them. Hard stepped inside, looking like a million dollars in cash and a century of power.

He was wearing a jet black three-piece suit by Brioni that hung perfectly off his frame, the fabric catching the restaurant's grand chandeliers with a faint, expensive sheen. Beneath the jacket, a stiff white Tom Ford collar framed his handsome face, but it was the tie that drew every eye in the room—a pleated Stefano Ricci silk the color of solid old gold, pinned down by a polished gold bar. A yellow-gold Rolex President gleamed from beneath his French cuffs as he adjusted his lapels. On his arm was Candy, looking every bit the queen to his king, matching his CEO aura with her own effortless elegance.

The sleek, low-lit host stand stood just ahead, backed by the sprawling, high-ceilinged expanse of the main dining room. The head host, sharply dressed young black man who'd been briefed well in advance for the private event, immediately stood up straighter as Hard approached.

The host didn't need check a book for Hard's name; he looked up, smiled with deep respect, and raised his voice just enough to cut through the ambient Jeremih song and the low chatter of the bar.

"Ladies and gentlemen, RPM Steak is honored to welcome home… Mr. Hardis Gaing!"

The announcement hit the room like a spark to gasoline.

Instantly, the low, excited noise of the restaurant was swallowed whole by a roaring wave of cheers, whistles, and thunderous applause. Looking out over the main floor, it seemed like half of Chicago had showed up. Hard's many friends, loyal associates, and extended family members were standing up from the plush leather booths, raising their cocktail glasses and shouting his name. The sheer volume of the love in the room vibrated right through the rich wood and cream-toned walls. Hard paused, a slow, knowing smile spreading across his face as he nodded to the crowd, soaking in a reception that felt less like a welcome home lunch and more like a coronation.

Cutting through the initial surge of the crowd came Pastor Gregory Newsome.

The Pastor was a striking figure himself, moving with a shepherd's easy grace and wearing a sharp, tailored suit that showed he knew how to carry himself in a place this nice. His face was lit up with a brilliant, spirit-filled smile as he extended a hand, firmly clasping Hard's before wrapping him in a brief, powerful half-hug.

"Welcome back, brotha Hard," Pastor Newsome said over the booming claps of applause, his deep, resonant voice carrying an undeniable warmth. "The Lord is good. I really mean it when I say it. God is good all the time. Come on up, everybody's been waiting on you."

With a gentle, guiding hand on Hard's shoulder, Pastor Newsome began leading him and Candy away from the main floor, steering them toward the flight of stairs that ascended to the stunning upper-level mezzanine. As they climbed, the panoramic view of the crowded restaurant opened up below them, the balcony-style private rooms of the mezzanine level waiting just ahead, packed tight with Hard's inner circle.

He saw Tone Bone with his wife, Candace Bostic, and their two teenage girls. Lorde and about a dozen other members of the Dark Side TVLs were in their own section, their eyes as cold as the ice cubes in their Styrofoam cups of

Lean. Baby Gang and his Money Gang clique were present, as were Flower, Vee, and their friends; Baby Gang and his guys had joined up with Hard's rapidly growing conglomerate of Vice Lords, so he'd been seeing a lot of them lately. There were high-ranking Vice Lords from every branch, as well as numerous Gangster Disciples, Black Disciples, New Breeds, Black Souls, Black P. Stones, and Mickey Cobras who'd come out to show their respects.

One person who really surprised Hard with his presence was Twista, the tongue-twisting rap legend who'd grown up on the same West Side streets as Hard.

Hard sat down next to Candy. He'd purposely skipped breakfast so he could have a ravenous appetite for the lunch, and he was ready to eat like a king.

The private mezzanine room at RPM Steak overlooked the buzzing, amber-lit dining floor below, but up here, tucked behind polished dark wood and heavy glass, the atmosphere was intimate. Hard felt like a married man sitting next to his beautiful wife. He a Glock 23 on his hip, which he hated carrying, and he had a team of bloodthirsty young Vice Lords watching his every move, which he didn't trust, but the fact remained that he felt better than he'd ever felt before, and he knew that feeling had everything to do with Tazera "Candy" Williams.

The waiters moved like ghosts, setting down a spread befitting a king's return. At the center of the table was a massive, 42-ounce Westholme Wagyu Tomahawk, thick-crusted from the oak-fired embers and sliced clean off the bone, its rich marbling glistening under the soft lighting. Next to it sat a pristine plate of thick-cut bacon glazed in bourbon-vanilla bean, a bowl of creamy White Cheddar Bacon Mac & Cheese, and RPM's famous Millionaire's Potato—a decadent, golden spud whipped with fontina and buried under a generous mountain of freshly shaved black truffles.

Hard took his time, savoring a perfectly medium-rare slice of the Wagyu. Beside him, Candy smiled, her eyes warm as she watched him finally relax, enjoying a luxury that didn't come out of a prison cafeteria or a Styrofoam container on the block.

Ten minutes later the heavy glass door clicked open.

Lorde and Tone Bone slipped into the room, their all-encompassing street aura instantly shifting the air in the room. Lorde was dressed to impress but still carried that restless, sharp-eyed energy of a drill rapper actively in the trenches. Tone Bone moved with the slow, deliberate confidence of a man who didn't need to wrap his hands around a gun anymore because his phone calls moved entire city blocks.

"Pops," Lorde said, stepping up to the table and nodding with profound respect. "Food look crazy. Glad to see you back at the table for real, though. On Neal. It's only up from here."

"Welcome home, big homie," Tone Bone added, pulling up a chair and resting his forearms on the backrest. "We just had to let the family have their moment downstairs first. But you know how it go. Business don't sleep for no man, definitely not for no street nigga."

Hard laid his gold-plated steak knife down on the rim of his plate. He didn't smile, but his eyes were sharp, calculating. "What's on your mind, son?"

Lorde leaned in closer, dropping his voice so it didn't carry past the booth. "Look, I got a line on some'n big. I'm talkin' about a real-life trap millionaire. It's this rapper I locked in with outta Akron, Ohio. He a real heavyweight out there, got his own money and a whole network touchin' Cleveland and Detroit. He's clean, he's hungry, and he's ready to buy twenty bricks right now. I told him it's $18,500 apiece, cash on delivery. We pull this off, that's $370,000 off a single play, Pops. And it sets up a whole new market for us to get money through."

Tone Bone grinned, a low, smooth chuckle escaping his throat as he checked his watch. "Man, the timing couldn't be better, Hard. That actually reminds me—I just got off the line with our people in Matamoros. The connect just touched down with a fresh shipment. They already sorted through the logistics, and I got another two hundred bricks sittin' in my girl's rental property out there in Harvey, just waiting for you whenever you're ready to greenlight that move. Between Akron and what we got goin' in the city, we could run the whole Midwest by the end of the summer."

Hard didn't answer right away. He leaned back in his leather chair, the dense silk of his gold Stefano Ricci tie shifting against his chest. He looked at Lorde, seeing the raw, dangerous hunger he used to have when he was young. He looked at Tone Bone, seeing a man completely entangled in the mechanics of a machine that only ever ground people down into dust.

Then, he looked over at Candy.

She wasn't looking at the food anymore. She was looking at him, her eyes quiet, holding a silent, heavy plea. She didn't say a word, but her hand gently found his under the table, her fingers wrapping tightly around his.

Two hundred more bricks. Twenty of them essentially already gone to Ohio. Millions of dollars floating in the air, just waiting for him to reach out and snatch it. But Hard's mind didn't see the cash. It saw the flashing blue lights. It saw the cold steel of a county jail bullpen. It saw the face of El Verdugo getting carried off to a federal supermax for three life sentences. It saw the graves of Thirty, Baby Lord, Terry Lee, and every other soldier who thought they could outrun the game. He'd already paid his debt to the state. He'd survived the streets, survived the joints, and here he was, sitting in a three-piece Brioni suit at RPM Steak with a beautiful woman who actually loved him for who he was, not what he dealt.

The street life was a carousel of trials and tribulations. It never ended until you were either dead or buried alive under a federal indictment.

Hard let out a slow, hesitant breath, shaking his head. The shiny gold of his Rolex caught the light as he raised his hand, waving the proposition away.

"Nah," Hard said, his voice flat, heavy, and final. "Take that Akron play if you want it, Lorde. Tone, you go ahead and hand them bricks to whoever wants to chase that check. But leave me out of it."

Lorde blinked, stunned. "Pops? You serious? That's a few million on the table."

"Yeah, and I'm done chasin' it," Hard said, turning his head to look directly at Candy, his grip tightening around her hand. "I spent my whole life lookin' over my shoulder, waiting for the front door to get kicked in or a window to get shot out. I got a good woman. I got my freedom. I'm living the quiet life now. Let them young niggas have the stress. I'm eating my steak."

Tone Bone and Lorde exchanged a long, silent look. They knew Hard well enough to know that when he spoke with that tone, there was no negotiating.

"Respect, bruh," Tone Bone said quietly, standing up and smoothing down his jacket. "You earned that retirement the gang way. I'm here if you ever need me."

As the two younger men exited the private room, leaving the door to click shut behind them, Candy let out a breath she felt like she'd been holding for years. She leaned over, pressing her forehead against Hard's navy-blue shoulder.

"You mean that?" she whispered.

Hard picked up his fork, a genuine smile finally breaking across his face. "Every word, baby. Now pass me that mac and cheese."

Epilogue: Blinded

Six Months Later

June, 2026

The summer heat was just beginning to bake the Chicago suburbs, but down in the basement of the Concord Vineyard house, the air was cool and crisp. Hard's man-cave was finally complete. The walls were lined with polished mahogany, a massive ledger-stone wet bar sat in the corner, and the ambient lighting threw a soft glow over the leather recliners.

Hard sat at a heavy oak desk, the quiet whir-whir-whir of a digital money counter filling the room. He was running $300,000 in crisp hundred-dollar bills through the machine—the last of his dirty money, a cushion for the quiet life. On his wrist, the gold Rolex President gleamed under the basement lights. He looked relaxed, a man completely insulated from the madness of the streets above.

Then, his iPhone buzzed against the wood. The screen read: HJ.

Hard picked it up, pressing it to his ear. "Yeah, son. What's the word?"

The voice on the other end didn't sound like a confident homicide detective. It sounded strained, heavy, and cracked with an icy rage.

"Pop," HJ said, his breathing shallow. "I found it. I found the file."

Hard sat up straighter, his hand dropping away from the stacks of cash. "What you talking about, HJ?"

"The murder you went down for," HJ spat, the words sounding like they carried the taste of venom. "I've been digging through old archives and cross-referencing state records from back then. Pop…it was Detective Maxie. The man who married my mama. The man who raised me after they put you in that cage." HJ paused, suffocating on his own realization. "He set you up. It wasn't a bad tip, and it wasn't sloppy police work. Maxie manufactured the evidence. He altered the timelines and buried the witness statements that cleared you. He did it all systematically, just to get you out of the picture so he could have Dominique for himself."

The basement suddenly felt freezing cold. Hard didn't blink. The diamond Cuban-link against his chest felt heavy. Every year he'd spent staring at a cinderblock wall, every milestone he'd missed with Nunu and his boys, flashed through his mind like a lightning strike. It hadn't been the game that beat him. It was a crooked cop playing God with his life for a woman.

. "What did your people say?" Hard asked, his voice dropping into a dangerously low register.

. "I took everything to my captain," HJ said, his voice trembling with a mixture of rage and disgust. "The whole paper trail. You know what that bastard told me? He looked me in my eye and told me I was 'blinded by blood.' He told me Maxie is retired law enforcement, a protected name, and that digging up thirty-year-old skeletons would destroy the department. He told me I need to choose the badge over my bloodline, or he'd strip me of my shield by Friday."

A long, agonizing silence hung on the line.

"Pop?" HJ asked quietly. "You there?"

"I'm here," Hard said. "Take care of yourself, son."

He hung up the phone.

The quiet peace of the Concord Vineyard house, the beautiful manicure of the lawn upstairs, the luxury of the Brioni suits and dapper tracksuits from Amiri and Sinew—it all evaporated in a single heartbeat. The illusion of the "quiet life" shattered. The system had stolen his youth, a cop had stolen his woman, and now the state was protecting the monster who did it. If the law wouldn't give him justice, the streets would give him power. He was done playing the retired gentleman.

Hard reached down, picked up his phone again, and dialed a number he'd promised himself he'd never again call.

Tone Bone answered on the second ring. "Yooooo, big homie. What's the word, beloved?"

"Them two hundred bricks," Hard said, his voice flat, emotionless, and cold as stone. "The ones sitting out in Harvey. If you still got 'em send 'em to me. All of 'em. We're running the whole Midwest."

On the other end, Tone Bone took a sharp breath, sensing the immediate shift in the universe. "Say less, big homie. They'll be in motion within the hour."

Hard stood up from the desk, leaving the $300,000 sitting under the amber lights of his man-cave. He walked up the basement stairs, his footsteps heavy and deliberate on the hardwood.

Candy was in the kitchen, organizing a vase of fresh summer flowers, looking up with a warm smile as she heard him approach. But the smile faded the moment she saw his eyes. The easy, relaxed man she'd eaten steak with at RPM Steak was gone. In his place stood the ruthless, calculating patriarch who had conquered the West Side of Chicago many years before.

Hard walked right up to her, his gaze locked onto hers.

"Baby," Hard said, his voice echoing in the quiet luxury of the kitchen, "it's time to get some real money. You ready to get rich? I mean rich-rich, so rich we could buy this whole subdivision?"

Candy smiled and walked to him. She pressed her hands flat against his powerful chest, rose up on tiptoe, and kissed him right on the mouth.

"Hard," she said, gazing longingly into his eyes, "I'm riding till the wheels fall off. Let's get to the bag."

TO BE CONTINUED

Lock Down Publications and Ca$h Presents Assisted Publishing Packages

Due to an increase in the price of services we have increased our prices. The prices below reflect the price increase as of 11/1/24.

BASIC PACKAGE	UPGRADED PACKAGE
$699 Editing Cover Design Formatting	**$1000** Typing Editing Cover Design Formatting Upload eBooks to Amazon Upload Paperback to Amazon
ADVANCE PACKAGE **$1,400** Typing Editing (line editing/content) Cover Design Formatting Copyright Registration Proofreading Upload eBooks to Amazon Upload Paperback to Amazon	**LDP SUPREME PACKAGE** **$1,700** Typing Editing (line editing/content) Cover Design Formatting Copyright Registration Proofreading Set up Amazon Account Upload eBooks to Amazon Upload Paperback to Amazon Advertise on LDP's Amazon and Facebook Page

***

Other services available upon request.
Additional charges may apply

Lock Down Publications
P.O. Box 944
Stockbridge, GA 30281-9998
Phone: 470 303-9761
Email: lockdownpublications@gmail.com

Submission Guideline

Submit the first three chapters of your completed manuscript to ldpsubmissions@gmail.com. In the subject line add **Your Book's Title**. The manuscript must be in a Word Doc file and sent as an attachment. Document should be in Times New Roman, double spaced, and in size 12 font. Also, provide your synopsis and full contact information. If sending multiple submissions, they must each be in a separate email.

Have a story but no way to send it electronically? You can still submit to LDP/Ca$h Presents. Send in the first three chapters, written or typed, of your completed manuscript to:

LDP: Submissions Dept
P.O. Box 944
Stockbridge, GA 30281-9998

DO NOT send original manuscript. Must be a duplicate. Provide your synopsis and a cover letter containing your full contact information.

Thanks for considering LDP and Ca$h Presents.

NEW RELEASES

BLOODLINE OF A SAVAGE 1-3
THESE VICIOUS STREETS 1-3
RELENTLESS GOON 1-3
SOULLESS GOON 1&2
BY PRINCE A. TAUHID

THE BUTTERFLY MAFIA 3
BY FUMIYA PAYNE

A THUG'S STREET PRINCESS 1&2
BY MEESHA

CITY OF SMOKE 1-3
BY MOLOTTI

GET IT IN SLUGS 1 &2
BY B. STALL

STANDING ON HER BUSINESS 1&2
BY DG SANTANA

STEPPERS 1,2&3
THE REAL BADDIES OF CHI-RAQ 1-3
BY KING RIO

THE LANE 1-3
BY KEN-KEN SPENCE

THUG OF SPADES 1&2
LOVE IN THE TRENCHES 1&2
CORNER BOYS 1&2
ONCE YOU GO GANGSTA
PROTÉGÉ OF A LEGEND 1- 3
BY COREY ROBINSON

TIL DEATH 3
BY ARYANNA

THE BIRTH OF A GANGSTER 4
BY DELMONT PLAYER

PRODUCT OF THE STREETS 1-3
BY DEMOND "MONEY" ANDERSON

MONEY HUNGRY DEMONS 1-2
BY TRANAY ADAMS

TRAP STARS
BY B. SHELLY

HUB CITY MENACE 1-4
BY J. WHITE

A THUGGISH PASSION 1&2
LAND OF DA HOOLIGANZ 1-4
KILLAZ ON STANDBY 1&2
FRESH OFF DA PORCH 1-3
SECURE DA BAG
AMBITIONS OF A SLIDER
FOR MY ENEMIES SAKE
SOULLESS GOON 1&2
FO'EVA ROLLIN 1-4
BY ASSA RAYMOND BAKER

THE LEVEL UP 1&2
BY LUXURY KING

HUNGRY FOR MONEY 1&2
SLIMBOS

DRILL CITY 1&2
BY ZAY'TOWVEN

QUEEN OF NAPTOWN 1&2
THA TAKEOVER 1-3
BY KEITH CHANDLER

LOVE ME OR LET ME GO
BY R. FACEY

SAVAGE DREAMZ
BY KING DAVID

MONEY AND DEAD HOMIES
BY DERRICK SUMMERS

A THUGS STREET PRINCESS 3 Coming Soon
BY MEESHA

BETRAYAL OF A G 2
BY RAY VINCI

SAVAGE FAMILY EMPIRE 1&2
SOULLESS GOON 1&2
THE DIRTY SIDE OF MONEY 1,2&3
BY PRINCE

BY THE TRUCKLOAD 1&2
TIPPIN' THE SCALES 1-4
BAD BITCHES WIT GUNZ 1-3
PROBLEM SOLVED 1-3
THE GIRLRILLA AND HER N*GGA
THE SINGLE LADIES
DYIN' TO GET RICH
THE GIRLRILLA AND HER N*GGA
BY CHRISTOPHER "DIESEL" HORNEZES

AVAILABLE NOW

RESTRAINING ORDER 1 & 2
BY CA$H & COFFEE

LOVE KNOWS NO BOUNDARIES 1-3
BY COFFEE

RAISED AS A GOON I, II, III & IV
BRED BY THE SLUMS I, II, III
BLAST FOR ME I & II
ROTTEN TO THE CORE I II III
A BRONX TALE I, II, III
DUFFLE BAG CARTEL I II III IV V VI
HEARTLESS GOON I II III IV V
A SAVAGE DOPEBOY I II
DRUG LORDS I II III
CUTTHROAT MAFIA I II
KING OF THE TRENCHES
BY GHOST

PUSH IT TO THE LIMIT
BY BRE' HAYES

LAY IT DOWN I & II
LAST OF A DYING BREED I II
BLOOD STAINS OF A SHOTTA I & II III
BY JAMAICA

LOYAL TO THE GAME I II III
LIFE OF SIN I, II III
BY TJ & JELISSA

IF LOVING HIM IS WRONG…I & II
LOVE ME EVEN WHEN IT HURTS I II III
BY JELISSA

BLOODY COMMAS I & II
SKI MASK CARTEL I, II & III
KING OF NEW YORK I II, III IV V
RISE TO POWER I II III
COKE KINGS I II III IV V
BORN HEARTLESS I II III IV
KING OF THE TRAP I II
BY T.J. EDWARDS

WHEN THE STREETS CLAP BACK I & II III
THE HEART OF A SAVAGE I II III IV
MONEY MAFIA I II
LOYAL TO THE SOIL I II III
BY JIBRIL WILLIAMS

A DISTINGUISHED THUG STOLE MY HEART I II & III
LOVE SHOULDN'T HURT I II III IV
RENEGADE BOYS 1-4
PAID IN KARMA 1-3
SAVAGE STORMS 1-3
AN UNFORESEEN LOVE 1-3
BABY, I'M WINTERTIME COLD 1-3
A THUG'S STREET PRINCESS 1,2&3
EMBRACING THE LOVE OF A BOSS 1&2
BY MEESHA

CUM FOR ME 1-8
AN LDP EROTICA COLLABORATION

WHEN A GOOD GIRL GOES BAD
BY ADRIENNE

BLOOD OF A BOSS 1-5
SHADOWS OF THE GAME
TRAP BASTARD
BY ASKARI

THE BIG HOMIE | KING RIO

A GANGSTER'S CODE 1-3
A GANGSTER'S SYN 1-3
THE SAVAGE LIFE 1-3
CHAINED TO THE STREETS 1-3
BLOOD ON THE MONEY 1-3
A GANGSTA'S PAIN 1-3
BEAUTIFUL LIES AND UGLY TRUTHS
CHURCH IN THESE STREETS
BY J-BLUNT

THE STREETS BLEED MURDER 1-3
THE HEART OF A GANGSTA 1-3
BY JERRY JACKSON

THE COST OF LOYALTY 1-3
BY KWELI

BRIDE OF A HUSTLA 1-3
THE FETTI GIRLS 1-3
CORRUPTED BY A GANGSTA 1-4
BLINDED BY HIS LOVE
THE PRICE YOU PAY FOR LOVE 1-3
DOPE GIRL MAGIC 1-3
BY DESTINY SKAI

A KINGPIN'S AMBITION
A KINGPIN'S AMBITION II
I MURDER FOR THE DOUGH
BY AMBITIOUS

WHITE BOYS 1&2
BY BANDEMIC

A DOPEBOY'S PRAYER
BY EDDIE "WOLF" LEE

THE KING CARTEL 1-3
BY FRANK GRESHAM

I RIDE FOR MY HITTA
I STILL RIDE FOR MY HITTA
BY MISTY HOLT

TRUE SAVAGE 1-7
DOPE BOY MAGIC 1-3
MIDNIGHT CARTEL 1-3
CITY OF KINGZ 1&2
NIGHTMARE ON SILENT AVE
THE PLUG OF LIL MEXICO 1&2
CLASSIC CITY
BY CHRIS GREEN

BACK IN BLOOD 1&2
SEX, MURDER AND GOD 1&2
COUNTDOWN OF A KILLA 1&2
GUNS DOWN, BOTTOMS UP 1&2
DEATH OF A SIDE CHICK
BY LO-LIFE

THESE NIGGAS AIN'T LOYAL 1-3
BY NIKKI TEE

GANGSTA SHYT 1-3
BY CATO

THE ULTIMATE BETRAYAL
BY PHOENIX

BOSS'N UP 1-3
BY ROYAL NICOLE

I LOVE YOU TO DEATH
BY DESTINY J

THE BIG HOMIE | KING RIO

LOVE & CHASIN' PAPER
BY QAY CROCKETT

TO DIE IN VAIN
SINS OF A HUSTLA
BY ASAD

A GANGSTER'S REVENGE 1-4
THE BOSS MAN'S DAUGHTERS 1-5
A SAVAGE LOVE 1&2
BAE BELONGS TO ME 1&2
A HUSTLER'S DECEIT 1-3
WHAT BAD BITCHES DO 1-3
SOUL OF A MONSTER 1-3
KILL ZONE
A DOPE BOY'S QUEEN 1-3
TIL DEATH 1-3
IMMA DIE BOUT MINE 1-6
DYING FOR LIKES 1&2
KILLA CREW 1&2
BY ARYANNA

BROOKLYN HUSTLAZ
BY BOOGSY MORINA

BROOKLYN ON LOCK 1 & 2
BY SONOVIA

GANGSTA CITY
BY TEDDY DUKE

THE STREETS ARE CALLING
BY DUQUIE WILSON

STEADY MOBBN' 1-3
THE STREETS STAINED MY SOUL 1-3
BY MARCELLUS ALLEN

A DRUG KING AND HIS DIAMOND 1-3
A DOPEMAN'S RICHES
HER MAN, MINE'S TOO 1&2
CASH MONEY HO'S
THE WIFEY I USED TO BE 1&2
PRETTY GIRLS DO NASTY THINGS
BY NICOLE GOOSBY

LIPSTICK KILLAH 1-3
CRIME OF PASSION 1-3
FRIEND OR FOE 1-3
BY MIMI

TRAPHOUSE KING 1-3
KINGPIN KILLAZ 1-3
STREET KINGS 1&2
PAID IN BLOOD 1&2
CARTEL KILLAZ 1-3
DOPE GODS 1&2
BY HOOD RICH

MARRIED TO A BOSS 1-3
BY DESTINY SKAI & CHRIS GREEN

WHO SHOT YA 1-3
SON OF A DOPE FIEND 1-4
HEAVEN GOT A GHETTO 1&2
SKI MASK MONEY 1&2
BY RENTA

FUK SHYT
BY BLAKK DIAMOND
GORILLAZ IN THE BAY 1-4
TEARS OF A GANGSTA 1/&2
3X KRAZY 1&2
STRAIGHT BEAST MODE 1&2
BY DE'KARI

TRIGGADALE 1-3
MURDA WAS THE CASE 1-3
BY ELIJAH R. FREEMAN

SLAUGHTER GANG 1-3
RUTHLESS HEART 1-3
BY WILLIE SLAUGHTER

KINGZ OF THE GAME 1-7
CRIME BOSS 1-4
BY PLAYA RAY

DON'T F#CK WITH MY HEART 1&2
BY LINNEA

GOD BLESS THE TRAPPERS 1-3
THESE SCANDALOUS STREETS 1-3
FEAR MY GANGSTA 1-5
THESE STREETS DON'T LOVE NOBODY 1-2
BURY ME A G 1-5
A GANGSTA'S EMPIRE 1-4
THE DOPEMAN'S BODYGAURD 1&2
THE REALEST KILLAZ 1-3
THE LAST OF THE OGS 1-3
BY TRANAY ADAMS

ADDICTED TO THE DRAMA 1-3
IN THE ARM OF HIS BOSS
BY JAMILA

LOYALTY AIN'T PROMISED 1&2
BY KEITH WILLIAMS

YAYO 1-4
A SHOOTER'S AMBITION 1&2
BRED IN THE GAME
BY S. ALLEN

THE BIG HOMIE | KING RIO

FOREVER GANGSTA 1&2
GLOCKS ON SATIN SHEETS 1&2
BY ADRIAN DULAN

TRAP GOD 1-3
RICH $AVAGE 1-3
MONEY IN THE GRAVE 1-3
CARTEL MONEY 1&2
BY MARTELL TROUBLESOME BOLDEN

TOE TAGZ 1-4
LEVELS TO THIS SHYT 1&2
IT'S JUST ME AND YOU
BY AH'MILLION

KINGPIN DREAMS 1-3
RAN OFF ON DA PLUG
BY PAPER BOI RARI

THE STREETS MADE ME 1-3
BY LARRY D. WRIGHT

CONFESSIONS OF A GANGSTA 1-4
CONFESSIONS OF A JACKBOY 1-3
CONFESSIONS OF A HITMAN
CONFESSIONS OF A DOPE BOY
BY NICHOLAS LOCK

CAUGHT UP IN THE LIFE 1-3
THE STREETS NEVER LET GO 1-3
BY ROBERT BAPTISTE

I'M NOTHING WITHOUT HIS LOVE
SINS OF A THUG
TO THE THUG I LOVED BEFORE
A GANGSTA SAVED XMAS
IN A HUSTLER I TRUST
BY MONET DRAGUN

THE BIG HOMIE | KING RIO

NEW TO THE GAME 1-3
MONEY, MURDER & MEMORIES 1-3
BY MALIK D. RICE

QUIET MONEY 1-3
THUG LIFE 1-3
EXTENDED CLIP 1&2
A GANGSTA'S PARADISE
BY TRAI'QUAN

THE STREETS WILL NEVER CLOSE 1-3
BY K'AJJI

CREAM 2-3
THE STREETS WILL TALK
BY YOLANDA MOORE

THE ULTIMATE SACRIFICE 1-6
KHADIFI
IF YOU CROSS ME ONCE 1-3
ANGEL 1-4
IN THE BLINK OF AN EYE
BY ANTHONY FIELDS

THE LIFE OF A HOOD STAR
BY CA$H & RASHIA WILSON

CONCRETE KILLA 1-3
VICIOUS LOYALTY 1-3
BLOODY MONEY BAGS 1&2
BY KINGPEN

NIGHTMARES OF A HUSTLA 1-3
BLOOD AND GAMES 1&2
BY KING DREAM

MONEY GAME 1&2
BY SMOOVE DOLLA

KILLA KOUNTY 1-5
TENDER 1&2
TREACHEROUS YN
BY KHUFU

LIFE OF A SAVAGE 1-4
A GANGSTA'S QUR'AN 1-4
MURDA SEASON 1-3
GANGLAND CARTEL 1-3
CHI'RAQ GANGSTAS 1-4
KILLERS ON ELM STREET 1-3
JACK BOYZ N DA BRONX 1-3
A DOPEBOY'S DREAM 1-3
JACK BOYS VS DOPE BOYS 1-3
COKE GIRLZ
COKE BOYS
SOSA GANG 1&2
BRONX SAVAGES
BODYMORE KINGPINS
BLOOD OF A GOON
BY ROMELL TUKES

HARD AND RUTHLESS 1&2
MOB TOWN 251
THE BILLIONAIRE BENTLEYS 1-3
REAL G'S MOVE IN SILENCE
BY VON DIESEL

MOB TIES 1-7
SOUL OF A HUSTLER, HEART OF A KILLER 1-3
GORILLAZ IN THE TRENCHES
OPPS CRY TOO 1-3
THE DAUGHTER OF A CARTEL BOSS 1&2
BY SAYNOMORE

FOR THE LOVE OF A BOSS 1&2
BY C. D. BLUE

THE BIG HOMIE | KING RIO

BODYMORE MURDERLAND 1-3
THE BIRTH OF A GANGSTER 1-4
TOP OF THE TRENCHES
BY DELMONT PLAYER

MOBBED UP 1-4
THE BRICK MAN 1-5
THE COCAINE PRINCESS 1-10
STEPPERS 1-3
SUPER GREMLIN 1-5
A GANGSTA'S SON
THE CONNECT'S SECRET
BY KING RIO

LOVE ME OR LET ME GO 1&2
BY R. FACEY

A GANGSTA'S KARMA 1-5
BY FLAME
BLOOD AND MAYHEM
BY JJ DORSEY
KING OF THE TRENCHES 1-3
By GHOST & TRANAY ADAMS

QUEEN OF THE ZOO 1&2
BY BLACK MIGO

GRIMEY WAYS 1-3
BETRAYAL OF A G
BY RAY VINCI

XMAS WITH AN ATL SHOOTER
BY CA$H & DESTINY SKAI

KING KILLA 1&2
PAPER, ROCK, SNAKES
BY VINCENT "VITTO" HOLLOWAY

THE BIG HOMIE | KING RIO

BETRAYAL OF A THUG 1&2
BY FRE$H

COUNTDOWN OF A KILLA 1&2
SEX, MURDER AND GOD 1&2
GUNS DOWN, BOTTOMS UP 1&2
BY LO-LIFE

FOR THE LOVE OF BLOOD 1-4
BY JAMEL MITCHELL

HOOD CONSIGLIERE 1-3
NO TIME FOR ERROR 1&2
REAL
BY KEESE

THE PLUG'S RUTHLESS DAUGHTER 1,2&3
REDEMPTION IN THE STREETS
BY TONY DANIELS

MOAN IN MY MOUTH
BY XTASY

BORN IN THE GRAVE 1-3
CRIME PAYS 1-3
By Self Made Tay

TORN BETWEEN A GANGSTER AND A GENTLEMAN
BY J-BLUNT

LOYALTY IS EVERYTHING 1-3
CITY OF SMOKE 1-3
BY MOLOTTI

HERE TODAY GONE TOMORROW 1&2
BY FLY ROCK

PILLOW PRINCESS
BY S. HAWKINS

WOMEN LIE MEN LIE 1-4
FIFTY SHADES OF SNOW 1-3
STACK BEFORE YOU SPLURGE
GIRLS FALL LIKE DOMINOES
NAÏVE TO THE STREETS
BY ROY MILLIGAN

THE BUTTERFLY MAFIA 1-3
SALUTE MY SAVAGERY 1&2
BY FUMIYA PAYNE

THE LANE 1&2
BY KEN-KEN SPENCE

THE PUSSY TRAP 1-5
BY NENE CAPRI

DIRTY DNA
BY BLAQUE

SANCTIFIED AND HORNY
BY XTASY

THE RUTHLESS LIFE
HIDEOUS
BY TOMMY COOK

BOOKS BY LDP'S CEO, CA$H

TRUST IN NO MAN
TRUST IN NO MAN 2
TRUST IN NO MAN 3
BONDED BY BLOOD
SHORTY GOT A THUG
THUGS CRY
THUGS CRY 2
THUGS CRY 3
TRUST NO BITCH
TRUST NO BITCH 2
TRUST NO BITCH 3
TIL MY CASKET DROPS
RESTRAINING ORDER
RESTRAINING ORDER 2
IN LOVE WITH A CONVICT
LIFE OF A HOOD STAR
XMAS WITH AN ATL SHOOTER

www.ingramcontent.com/pod-product-compliance
Lightning Source LLC
LaVergne TN
LVHW030911080826
845145LV00010B/2853

* 9 7 8 1 9 7 1 7 7 0 3 0 7 *